Elsewhere, Home

Leila Aboulela

Elsewhere, Home

Black Cat
New York

First published in Great Britain in 2018 by Telegram Books

Published simultaneously in Canada
Printed in the United States of America

First Grove Atlantic edition: February 2019

ISBN 978-0-8021-2913-0
eISBN 978-0-8021-4694-6

Library of Congress Cataloging-in-Publication data is available for this title.

Black Cat
an imprint of Grove Atlantic
154 West 14th Street
New York, NY 10011

Distributed by Publishers Group West

groveatlantic.com

18 19 20 21 10 9 8 7 6 5 4 3 2 1

Contents

Summer Maze

It was not her first time boarding the Egypt Air flight from Heathrow to Cairo. Nadia's life was a zigzag of these annual visits that sometimes stretched into every single day of the holidays and made the September return to school feel abrupt and unfocused. She had made sure to pack the PlayStation but it might not be enough. Her mother's bulky arm pressed against her. Lateefa was in her best clothes but Nadia wasn't. They had argued about this.

The airplane was going to be full and there was a mix up over the seating arrangements. Nadia watched the steward struggle in his broken English to remove a couple from seats which their boarding cards indicated to be rightly theirs. He pronounced every 'p' as a 'b' so that it was, 'Blease this is seat 3D'. Just like my mother, Nadia thought. The next challenge taken up by the crew was to find enough storage space for the hand baggage of the Egyptian passengers. Big, bulging plastic bags testified to suitcases that were unable to hold any more, filled to the brim with the results of shopping. Like my mother, Nadia thought.

For weeks Lateefa had walked up and down Oxford Street, searching for the best bargains, tightly clutching her receipts in fear that she would lose them. She would buy, exchange and agonise over every purchase. Wearing her Dr Scholl exercise slippers (because her feet always got swollen from too much walking) she would stand in the queue of Marks and Spencer's Customers Services, tense, never quite believing that they would refund her money. She would hand in her receipt, crumpled from the sweat of her palms, and nervously explain her reasons to the bored sales assistant. And Nadia, if she was with her, would feel ashamed, not only from the slippers but from the furtive look in her mother's eyes.

It was happening again, and it was one of Nadia's anxieties about the summer. The air hostess was addressing her in Arabic and she could not answer. She turned to her mother and Lateefa not only translated but answered the stewardess, 'No, we won't give up either of our seats; we are together.' There was a time when Nadia had spoken Arabic, her baby chatter, her first fumbling words. But then with starting nursery school, the language had started to evade her. Not overnight of course. There was a time when she understood but would only answer in English, slyly, eager to hurt her mother. And then finally came the time when she could understand a little but could not speak fluently. Yet there remained within her a faint memory of a complete closeness with Lateefa, a time of unqualified approval that was somehow lost with her ability to speak her mother's tongue.

In Cairo she was a stranger, but a stranger who went unnoticed, who was not tricked into paying extra for taxi rides and souvenirs. The effect was like a disguise, a role she was playing in an overworld which did not demand from her much skill or strategy. She could not really think of herself as Egyptian, nor did she want to. The city's traffic overwhelmed her, the cars weaving in and out of the lanes, the pedestrians crossing in the middle of the road, the overflowing buses. She would stare unnerved at the sight of a woman riding on the back seat of a motorcycle with a child balanced on her lap. On every trip she would long for London and promise herself she would not come again. She would tell herself that she was not a child any more, some of her friends no longer went with their families on holiday – she could do the same. But perhaps it was her mother's anger that she feared, the hot reckless words like sandpaper on skin. Or perhaps she was bewitched by the welcome that she received from her aunt and cousins.

In England her friends' lives were a smooth continuation of their parents' or so it seemed to her. When they made Valentine's cards at school, their mothers understood; when they dressed up for Halloween, their mothers helped.

But Lateefa would not understand, 'You wasted good time at school making cards!' 'Those silly beoble telling their children the bresents came from Santa Claus. How will they learn to be grateful that their fathers and mothers get them nice things?' Lateefa's words would stay in Nadia's mind, echoing, though she tried hard to push them away. She could see things in the 'normal' way, the same way that her friends did, untainted by Lateefa's judgments. But she could also change the lens and see what her mother saw. It was as if Lateefa's values were a subtle, throttled part of her. She had sucked them down with her mother's milk.

Her cousin, Khalid, was waiting to meet them, leaning against the iron railing that separated the emerging passengers from the car park. The Khalid of each and every summer, old enough to be intriguing, young enough to be her only Cairo friend. She aimed her trolley at him and began to walk faster. 'It's so hot,' she said to her mother but Lateefa, surging ahead, didn't hear.

Although it was midnight, the airport was as busy as ever. Large tourist buses were parked in the open-air car park amidst the taxis that worked with meters and the posh 'limousines' which charged higher rates. The drivers had spilled out of their vehicles and were shouting, 'Taxee! Taxee!' into the dense crowd of tourists. They were aggressive and persistent, a few of them reaching to grab Nadia's trolley. She kept shaking her head. She kept saying, 'Thanks, but no we don't need a taxi.'

'Just ignore them,' Lateefa yelled back as if this was the easiest thing in the world. She was the one who reached Khalid first, beaming and hugging him, pulling his neck down to kiss his forehead and cheeks. 'You still haven't shaved your beard?' she scolded. 'One of these days you'll be arrested for a terrorist!'

He laughed and turned to shake Nadia's hand. When she was younger she had sat on his lap in cars and cinemas; in swimming pools she had wrapped slippery legs around his waist and squealed, 'Again! Again!' when he lifted her up from under her arms and threw her in the water. But that was a long time ago when he was a schoolboy and she was a child and the age gap between them had seemed large. For the past few years though, she had felt shy in his presence, especially in the first few days of the visit.

Khalid had prepared for the assault of their suitcases on the carrying capacity of his Lada. He had attached a metal frame to its roof and Nadia imagined him doing that after finishing work in the pharmacy, in the midst of moving out of his room, packing some clothes and climbing the three flights of stairs to share a room with his sister's children. His sister, her husband and their three children lived in a two-bedroom flat in the same building. It would be his home for the coming months while Nadia and Lateefa occupied his room downstairs. Khalid's room and sleeping in his bed were part of the rituals of the summer. Lateefa on a mattress on the floor which she rolled up in the morning and put on top of the bed. Then

Nadia waking late to the din from the street below and the smell of cooking, making her way through the crowded, elaborate furniture, towards her aunt's voice. Her aunt Salwa absorbed everyone's news and concerns; she was like an octopus reaching out for all her relations. Especially to Khalid's sister and her life in that more modern upstairs flat; her children's ailments, even her husband's problems at work seeped and overflowed down the three flights of stairs and into Aunt Salwa's home.

'What took you so long? You were almost the last passengers to come out.' Khalid fastened a rope on top of the suitcases so they would not fall off.

They were late because of a scene that had taken place in the customs hall. Fingering their green Egyptian passports, lifting their suitcases off the trolley to test their weight, a lanky custom's official told them to stand aside and open the suitcases for inspection. The weight of their bags had filled him with the suspicion that they were bringing in goods to sell in Egypt without paying custom duties. After keeping them waiting for half an hour, he demanded that every item be taken out, examined, priced and eventually taxed. Lateefa explained that all the things in the bags were gifts. The man listened unmoved as if he had heard all this before. He turned instead to wave through a group of tourists, bestowing upon them deferential smiles.

Whisking out their two British passports from her handbag, Lateefa waved them under the official's nose. 'If we had come into the country with *these*,' she shouted, 'you would not have treated us in this way! For a whole year I have not come home and this is the treatment I get. You treat foreigners better!' There were reasons, other than Lateefa's patriotic sentiments, why they left London on their British passport and entered Egypt with their Egyptian ones. It saved them £20 each, the cost of the visa, and it saved them the inconvenience, in Cairo, of registering themselves at the nearest police station as all foreigners had to do. The burgundy booklets worked liked magic. The custom official cleared his throat, 'Calm down Madam, we don't want you to come into Cairo so upset, have a nice stay.'

Lateefa narrated this to Khalid, with embellishments and a few gentle additions from Nadia. At a traffic light, cars bumper to bumper, a hand scraped Nadia's window. A man with no legs, on what she could only think of as a skateboard, was meandering through the cars. She gasped and cringed back from the face, just the ravaged face, suddenly appearing at the window. Lateefa glanced back at her and smiled, 'The spoilt young lady from Europe.' The nails scratched on to Khalid's window. Unperturbed he dropped a note without even turning to look at the man who clattered away to another car. Khalid and Lateefa continued their conversation, 'The sons of donkeys,' he chuckled. 'They probably wanted you to bribe your way out of customs.' In the back seat, Nadia fought back nausea and tears. That roaming, wanting man, half-human, half-skateboard, would feature in her nightmares.

On the next day, when Khalid came home from work,

he took Nadia aside and said, 'You and I are going on a special outing. Tonight you're going to meet my fiancée!' He laughed when Nadia squealed in surprise. 'Believe me,' he said. 'This summer is going to be completely different!'

Nadia had met other Egyptian girls before, distant relatives, family friends. She would find herself thrown in their company, hardly understanding what they were saying, shy and out of place. They would be polite to her but friendships never developed and she would always feel weary after such encounters, resentful of another of Lateefa's attempts to find companions for her. But Reem was different. And what was pivotal about her was that she spoke English. From the very first words, Nadia was drawn in. 'I've heard so much about you. Khalid told me about the time he visited you in London.' Everything was out in the open and clear. Nadia could talk back; she did not need to grapple with mouthfuls of Arabic words or run translations through her head.

Reem spoke English even with Khalid for she had been born in Oklahoma and lived there until she was twelve. When she came to Cairo, she went to the American School in Maadi, the CAC, and the AUC, the American University in Cairo, where she was now studying Islamic Architecture. It became the custom during that summer that whenever Khalid visited Reem or took her out – which was nearly every evening – Nadia would be with him. It was Reem who insisted on Nadia's presence, wanting to please her, to show her more of Cairo. So Nadia would sit in the back seat of the Lada, Reem in the front next to Khalid, sitting twisted on her seat so that she could talk to them both at the same time.

In a faintly Southern accent intersected here and there with Arabic words, Reem talked about how cool Khalid was, what a drag a few of her lectures were, and how awesome some of Cairo's mosques were. While scarves and long sleeves looked drab and old-fashioned on Lateefa, on Reem they looked fashionable. Loose fishermen trousers, colourful embroidered shirts, a gypsy-like scarf tied around her head, another rectangular transparent one on top with its two ends falling to her waist, and long sparkling earrings framing her face. Lateefa didn't seem to warm to Reem but when she wore skinny jeans and an oversized 'I Live to Shop' t-shirt, Nadia smiled, thinking about how much that logo suited her mother.

Reem did take Nadia shopping, in all the new air-conditioned stores that Cairo had to offer – Benetton, Mobacco, Stefanel – and Nadia was pleased that she could buy things so much cheaper than they were in London. This was not Lateefa's Cairo; this was a Cairo which offered spin classes, McDonalds, and a Pizza Hut where Nadia could order the 'Suber Subreme' because the pepperoni was beef.

Reem gave her a street map, unusual in that it was in English with cartoon-like drawings of the landmarks and the Nile. So Nadia would sit in the back seat of the Lada, the map spread out in front of her, feeling as if she were in a video adventure, navigating and lurching through a virtual maze, bit by bit unlocking the access to new areas of the game world. 'You're going the wrong way Khalid, this is a one-way street', she would shout. And when it didn't matter, she learnt to laugh too.

They went one afternoon together to the pyramids. 'Let's climb up,' Reem said when they arrived and she managed a few of the blocks of the largest pyramid before sitting down. Khalid climbed and sat next to her, while Nadia remained on the bottom block, making patterns in the desert sand with her feet. It was the best time of day to visit the pyramids, the sun no longer blinding but a giant orange button slipping on the horizon. A few camels carrying tourists bobbed across the desert, small boys pulled donkeys and offered rides. A family was picnicking, with a large watermelon, and kofta sandwiches wrapped in newspaper. A little girl with torn shoes and scruffy hair sold them roasted watermelon seeds and peanuts.

'Khalid, get us some peanuts, please,' said Reem. But he did not have to move for the girl, sensing the opportunity to sell, clambered up the stones to where they were sitting.

'Here Nadia, for you,' and Reem tossed her a wrap of peanuts before Nadia had time to say that she didn't want any.

Nadia saw an elderly couple, obviously tourists, walk towards the Sphinx. The woman reminded Nadia of her primary school dinner lady. The couple's advance was interrupted by a young boy selling small leather camels.

His faded t-shirt hovered above his navel and his left foot dragged a torn pair of sandals. He twisted himself around them, trying to get them to notice his wares though the couple showed no interest. But he persisted as if he had been taught that this was what he must do to sell.

'Look dear,' Nadia heard the woman say to her husband, 'He's selling them for a pound each and in the hotel they're five pounds!'

The accent made Nadia homesick for London. She moved towards the couple, drawn to their familiar tones, eager for a flicker of recognition, an encouragement to say hello. But when they looked up at her they saw someone different from them, an Egyptian girl at the foot of that large pyramid in Giza. Nadia forced herself to speak out because she needed this encounter now, needed to make this link. She said, 'If you haggle with him, you can even get two camels for a pound. He'll sell them to you for that price, if you stand your ground.' She illustrated by using her rudimentary Arabic on the boy. He immediately dropped his price to a local rate. The couple were delighted. 'And you speak such good English too!'

Nadia explained that she was from North London and chatted for a few minutes with Dan and Sheila from Tunbridge Wells. They were seasoned travellers having been to Greece, Israel and Jordan, but Cairo had more to offer, they said.

She walked back to Reem and Khalid feeling refreshed. The English couple were Londoners like her; she could speak their language and warm to their moods. But she was not a tourist and for her Egypt could never be a holiday destination like Jordan or Greece. Desert, pyramids and Sphinx were embedded in her DNA. They were her heritage whether she wanted it or not. In a few weeks' time she would go back to school and this time she would have something to say about what she did on her holidays. She would not be ashamed like every year before.

In this particular summer, though, Lateefa was quick to complain. Watching Nadia get dressed to go out to dinner, she said, 'Don't you think you're spending too much time with Khalid and Reem?'

'They've asked me to go along.'

'They're just being bolite.'

'No. Reem is not like that. She would be honest with me. If she wanted to be alone with Khalid she would tell me so.' But Nadia remembered a previous summer's conversation with her mother, when she had asked, 'Why do people in Egypt lie all the time? When Tante Salwa has visitors why does she always tell them to stay longer when they get up to leave? She goes on and on and she doesn't mean it, she wants them to go and she's relieved when they go.'

'It's bolite,' Lateefa had answered, 'and the visitors know that and they leave just the same.' This was Egyptian etiquette; these were the Egyptian complexities Nadia would never appreciate.

Now, she slipped her shoes on and refused to meet her

mother's eyes. 'I want to go out with them. Today we're going to TGI Fridays and it's on a boat on the Nile!'

'Make sure you pay for your own meal,' grumbled Lateefa. 'I don't want you to be unwanted and I certainly don't want you taking favours. I'd rather you didn't go at all.'

'Why are you doing this?' Nadia's voice rose. 'You are so annoying. You drag me here every summer against my will and when I finally start to enjoy myself you want to spoil everything!'

Later that evening, in order to make amends, Nadia joined her mother in front of the television. She asked her about the film, knowing that watching Arabic films together, while Lateefa translated, was a pastime her mother enjoyed. 'It's not really one of the best,' Lateefa now said. 'But it is bringing back memories. Your father and I watched it at the Cinema Normandy when we were engaged. Khalid came with us as a chaperone.' She laughed. 'He was seven years old. And every time we went out we had to take him with us! Your father struggled to amuse him and keep him occupied so that we could be together longer.'

Her mother was explaining why Khalid meant so much to her and why his engagement to Reem was her own personal loss. She had always hoped that he would choose Nadia even though Nadia had told her time and again that marrying one's cousin was gross!

The next day Reem took Nadia with her to the AUC

campus while Khalid was at work. They drank iced juice in the cafe and it felt different to be with Reem alone. There was an easy mood to the campus, the hairdos of the girls to look at, young men with bright eyes and loud voices. Nadia glimpsed the corner of a tennis court, the thud of a racket and a cheer. It must be fun to play tennis in the open air, skipping classes but not going home. She would like to come to this oasis again, with its high walls that kept the city's pollution and noise at a distance.

Reem was asking, 'Is your mother still upset about our engagement?' She knew everything that was going on in Khalid's family.

Nadia shrugged, 'This summer she's not as happy as usual.'

'And what about you?'

'Oh, I'm on your side. I think you're perfect for each other.'

Reem smiled, 'You'll marry someone from London. I'm sure of it. There are other Muslims there, aren't there? Besides you're so young, you still have to do your exams and go to college.'

'I never said I wanted to get married. It's all my mum's idea.'

'She sounds like a real worrier. It's to be expected. An immigrant is a parent who finds out too late that she's given up her child for adoption.'

'But she'll fight it all the way,' Nadia sighed. 'She tugs and keeps me close.'

Reem smiled, 'My parents brought me back here to Cairo because they were anxious too. I was thirteen and I hated moving. It was difficult at first but now I think I'm better for having come here. Cairo teaches you every day. It makes you sharp because it's real and in your face.'

'I used to hate it,' Nadia said. The confession gave her a surge of confidence. She finished the rest of her orange juice and it was time for the campus tour.

In the bookshop Reem asked her, 'Have you read Naguib Mahfouz?' and there were his books translated into English. It was the first time for Nadia to see Arabic Literature translated into clear, familiar English. She picked up a novel by a Lateefa Al-Zayyat. And there were folk tales and fables from all over the Arab world. This was a treasure. This was a level-up. She spent all the money she had with her on books; short stories by Salwa Bakr, *The Mountain of Green Tea* and *The Thief and the Dogs*. For the first time her mother's life and words were there in front of her eyes, in solid black print, the English words evoking a sudden, startling credibility.

In the following mornings until the end of the summer, Nadia would sit in 'their' room, Khalid's room, not with her PlayStation but with the new books and the map of Cairo. The room, with its large brown desk and heavy wooden bed, held many childhood memories. Year after year, it seemed, she would come and find Khalid studying for his secondary school or university exams. He would sit at the same desk she was sitting on now, in his pyjama trousers and vest, his notes and papers spread before him. Although she was told by her Tante Salwa not to disturb him, she would sneak in when she found the door open. She would look at the pictures on his tapes and sometimes he would give her a paper and a pencil to scribble on while she lay on her stomach on the bed. He would ask her 'Where do you think the exam will come from?' and she would skim through his notes, pretending to understand and then stab a page at random. And he would say, 'I hope you're right, this is the easy bit.' Once he wrote a note for her to take to Tante Salwa in the kitchen. 'A student died today from extreme hunger,' the note said, 'because his mother forgot to feed him.' Tante Salwa laughed and made huge omelette sandwiches which Nadia carefully carried. Later when Tante Salwa came to collect the empty plate, Khalid put his arms around her waist, his head against her large stomach and said, 'Pray for me Mama.' And while Salwa said a prayer for him, Nadia too put her arms around her aunt and breathed in Salwa's perfume and kitchen scents.

* * *

I cry when Salwa tells me about Khalid's engagement. We are sitting in the kitchen with the tea tray between us, the smells of coriander and garlic. She tries to break the news to me softly, saying that nothing is formalised yet. But I know it is final and I am already broken with disappointment. She puts her arms around me close trying to calm me down, 'Nadia will marry better than him, wait, be patient; they are not meant for each other. The age gap between them is too big for these modern times.'

'Didn't we always speak about their betrothal, didn't you promise me?'

She sighs, 'I was wrong. Things have changed and young people make their own choices nowadays. Khalid and Reem are in love and want to be together. How can I stand in his way? And Nadia is still so young! Why are you in a hurry?'

I am alone in my sorrow. Salwa can't understand the fears that haunt a Muslim woman bringing up children in the West. Did her daughter's school friends ever speak of 'dad's girlfriend' in a matter-of-fact way? Did she ever go into shops where naked breasts and backs glared down from magazine racks, above the heads of small children buying sweets? Did she pass people who kissed and touched in parks and bus stops without shame? If you stare at them, they will look back with vacant, uncomprehending eyes, a weird kind of innocence. When people wed in the West, I tell Salwa, they would have tried each other out first, the way a worker is given employment on a trial basis!

I talk to Salwa but how can she imagine the long continuous silence, where no one speaks out and says this is wrong and forbidden? I have to bring Nadia up and keep her protected and warm like a plant in a glass house, seeing the grey world outside through the transparent panes without being thrashed by hail and cut by frost. Growing up untouched by sin and chaos, but not hidden from it. Understanding its danger and keeping herself apart.

'Yes, I want her to marry young,' I say. 'Because there is protection in marriage. And Khalid is my first choice.'

'I wish that you and Hamdy had stayed in Egypt,' Salwa hands me a tissue. She pours me a glass of tea. 'By going away you have become more old-fashioned. Things here are not as conventional and innocent as in our youth. Parents no longer control their children or even know what they are up to! Lateefa *habibti,* you are lagging behind. It is as if, by being away, time stood still for you!'

For my blinding headache I take two aspirins and fall asleep, only waking up when Nadia comes home from her outing with Khalid. Her happy face lightens my spirits. She has been told the news and is eager to meet the new bride, asking if we will come from London for the wedding.

'I hope their engagement breaks up,' I say. 'I hope he comes to his senses and marries you instead.'

'In your dreams,' she moves away from me.

Maybe she had said this before but I am now hearing her for the first time. Using that word 'gross' and making faces. This aversion to cousins marrying is something the English taught her, something a girl brought up in Egypt would not feel.

Once again we board the airplane that will take us back to London. Nadia sits next to me on the aisle seat and busies herself reading. What am I taking her back to? Her father and I took the decision to make London our home and now we will reap what we sowed. I feed on my fear as if it will protect me from what I dread most. In London I pass laments back and forth with other mothers. Flailing around in a maze, we swap stories of dead-ends. Someone's son converted to Christianity, another's daughter works in a bar and even that studious boy turned out to belong to a terrorist group. 'Bad friends are the root,' I am warned. 'Marry her off,' is a common piece of advice. Well, this summer was certainly a marriage scheme gone wrong!

I look down at the book Nadia is holding and I am surprised to see my first name written in English on the cover. She explains that she is reading an English translation of *The Open Door*. 'I am going to spend my gap year in Cairo learning Arabic. Properly. Well enough to read a book,' she says.

My immediate reaction is joy which I must hide lest she abandons the idea to spite me. 'I could teach you to read and write Arabic,' I say. 'You don't need to go anywhere.'

'Yes, I do.' She frowns. 'No one spends their gap year sitting at home with their mother.'

'What is this gab year anyway?'

'Gap, gap with a p.'

'Gabp'

'No. Say 'p', like in pee pee! You can certainly say 'pee' properly and then in every other word change it to a 'b'! It's daft.'

I laugh because she cares about a stupid word, because maybe, after all, there is hope. We are ready to fly now. Nadia pushes her table up, puts her book away and fastens her seatbelt. She takes my hand and I am touched to tears by her gesture. I start to speak but the pilot is saying something as he begins the take-off. He says, 'In the name of Allah, the Compassionate, the Merciful,' as if to himself, under the roar of the engines.

Something Old,
Something New

Her country disturbed him. It reminded him of the first time he had held a human bone, the touching simplicity of it, the strength. Such was the landscape of Khartoum; bone-coloured sky, a purity in the desert air, bareness. A bit austere and therefore static. But he was driven by feelings, that was why he was here, that was why he had crossed boundaries and seas, and now walked through a blaze of hot air from the airplane steps to the terminal. She was waiting for him outside the airport, wearing national dress, a pale orange tobe that made her appear even more slender than she was. I mustn't kiss you. No, she laughed, you mustn't. He had forgotten how vibrant she was, how happy she made him feel. She talked, asked him questions. Did you have a good trip, are you hungry, did all your luggage arrive, were they nice to you in customs, I missed you too. There was a catch in her voice when she said that; in spite of her confidence she was shy. Come, come and meet my brother. They began to walk across a car park that was disorganised and dusty, the sun gleaming on the cars.

Her brother was leaning against a dilapidated Toyota. He was lanky with a hard-done-by expression. He looked irritated. Perhaps by the conflicting desire to get his sister off his hands and his misgivings about her marrying a foreigner. How did he see him now, through those narrow eyes, how did he judge him? A European coming to shake his hand, murmuring *salamu alleikum*, predictably wearing jeans, a white shirt, but somewhat subdued for a foreigner.

She sat in the front next to her brother. He sat in the back with the rucksack that wouldn't fit in the boot. The car seats were shabby, a thin film of dust covered everything. I will get used to the dust, he told himself, but not the heat. He could do with a breath of fresh air, that tang of rain he was accustomed to. He wanted her to be next to him. And it suddenly seemed to him, in a peevish sort of way, unfair that they should be separated like that. She turned her head back and looked at him, smiled as if she knew. He wanted to say, you have no idea how much I ache for you, you have no idea. But he could not say that, not least because the brother understood English.

It was like a ride in a funfair. The windows wide open; voices, noises, car-horns, people crossing the road at random, pausing in the middle, touching the cars with their fingers as if the cars were benign cattle. Any one of these passers-by could easily punch him through the window, yank off his watch, his sunglasses, snatch his wallet from the pocket of his shirt. He tried to roll up the window but couldn't. She turned and said, it's broken, I'm sorry. Her calmness made him feel that he needn't be so nervous. A group of schoolboys walked on the pavement, one of them stared at him, grinned and waved. He became aware that everyone looked like her, shared her colour, the women were dressed like her and they walked with the same slowness which had seemed to him exotic when he had seen her walking in Edinburgh.

Everything is new for you; she turned and glanced at him gently. The brother said something in Arabic.

The car moved away from the crowded market to a wide shady road. Look, she said, take off your sunglasses and look. There's the Nile.

And there was the Nile, a blue he had never seen before, a child's blue, a dream's blue. Do you like it? she asked. She was proud of her Nile.

Yes, it's beautiful, he replied. But as he spoke he noticed that the river's flow was forceful, not innocent, not playful. Crocodiles no doubt lurked beneath the surface, hungry and ruthless. He could picture an accident; blood, death, bones.

And here is your hotel, she said. I booked you into the Hilton.

She was proud that her country had a Hilton.

The car swept up the drive. A porter in a gaudy green uniform and stiff turban opened the door for him before he could do it himself. (In any case the car had been in an accident and the dented door could only be opened from outside). The porter took his rucksack; there was a small fuss involving the brother in order to open the boot and get the suitcase. His luggage was mostly presents for her family. She had told him on the phone what to get and how much to get. They would be offended, she had explained, if you come empty-handed, they would think you don't care for me enough.

The hotel lobby was impressive, the cool tingling blast of the air-conditioner, music playing, an expanse of marble. He felt soothed somehow, more in control after the bumpy ride. With the brother away to park the car and a queue at the reception desk, they suddenly had time to talk.

I need an exit visa, she explained, to be able to leave and go back with you. To get the exit visa, I have to give a reason for leaving the country.

Because you're my wife, he said and they smiled at the word.

Will be my wife. Will be *inshallah*.

Inshallah.

That's it, she said, we won't be able to get married and just leave. We'll have to stay a few days till the papers get sorted out. And the British Embassy ... that's another story.

I don't understand what the problem is, he said.

Oh, she sighed, people have a wedding and they go off on their honeymoon. But we won't be able to do that, we will have to hang around and run from the Ministry of Interior to the Passport office to the British Embassy.

I see, he said, I see. Do I need an exit visa?

No, you're a visitor, you can leave whenever you like. But I need a visa, I need a reason to leave.

Right.

They looked at each other and then he said, I don't think your brother likes me.

No, no, he doesn't mean to be unfriendly ... you'll see.

* * *

The first time he saw her was at the Sudanese restaurant near the new mosque in Edinburgh. His old chemistry teacher had taken him there after Friday prayers. When she brought the menu, she said to them that the peanut soup was good, a speciality, but his teacher wanted the hummus salad and he ordered the lentil soup instead because it was familiar. He was by nature cautious, wanting new things but held back by a vague mistrust. It was enough for the time being that he had stepped into the Nile Café, he had no intention of experimenting with weird tastes.

He was conscious of her footsteps as she came from

the kitchen, up the stairs. She was wearing trousers and a brown headscarf that was tied at the back of her neck. She had very black eyes that slanted. After that day he went to the Nile Café alone and often. It was convenient, close to the Department of Zoology where he worked as a lab technician. He wondered if, as she leant and put the dish of couscous in front of him, she could smell the chemicals on him.

They got talking because there weren't many customers in the restaurant and she had time on her hands. The restaurant was new and word had not yet got round that it was good.

We've started to get a few people coming in from the mosque, she told him. Friday especially is a good day.

Yes, it was a Friday when I first came here and met you. She smiled in a friendly way.

He told her that at one time he had not known that the big building next to the restaurant was a mosque. There was no sign that said so. I thought it was a church, he said, and she laughed and laughed. He left her an extra tip that day; it was not often that people laughed at his jokes.

Had it not been for his old chemistry teacher he would never have gone to the mosque. At a bus stop, a face he had not seen for a number of years. A face associated with a positive feeling, a time of encouragement. Secondary school, the ease with which he had written lab reports. They recognised each other straight away. How are you? What are you doing now? You were my best student.

In primary and secondary school, he had been the brightest in his class, the most able. He sat for the three sciences in his Standard Grades and got three As. It was the same when he did his Highers. There was no reason at all, his teachers said, why he should not sail through medical school. But he got to his third year in medicine and failed, failed again and dropped out. He had counselling and his parents were supportive, but no one really ever understood what had gone wrong. He was as bewildered by his failure as everyone else was. His get-up-and-go had suddenly disappeared, as if amputated. What's it all for, what's the point? he asked himself. He asked himself the taboo questions. And really, that was the worst of it, these were the questions that brought all the walls down.

Snap out of it, he was told. And snap out of it he eventually did, a girlfriend helped but then she found a job in London and drifted away. He was simply not up to medical school. It's a shame, everyone agreed. They were sympathetic but at the same time they labelled him now, they put him in a box; a student who had 'dropped out', a 'giver-upper'.

One day when she brought him his plate of aubergine and mincemeat he asked her, would you like to go up Arthur's Seat? She had never been there before. It was windy, a summer wind that carried away the hats of tourists and messed up people's hair. Because her hair was covered, she looked neat, slightly apart from everyone else. It made the outing not as carefree as he imagined it would. She told him she had recently got divorced after six months of marriage. She laughed when she said six months not six years, but he could tell she was sore – it was in her eyes. You have beautiful eyes, he said.

Everyone tells me that, she replied. He flushed and looked away at the green and grey houses that made up Edinburgh. She had wanted to talk about her divorce, she had not wanted to hear compliments.

They talked a little about the castle. He told her about his girlfriend, not the nice one who had gone down south, but the previous one who had dumped him. He was able to laugh about it now.

She said her husband had married her against his will. Not against her will, she stressed, but his will. He was in love with an English girl but his family disapproved and stopped sending the money he needed to continue his studies in Edinburgh. They thought a Sudanese girl like her would make him forget the girlfriend he had been living with. They were wrong. Everything went wrong from day one. It's a stupid story, she said, her hands in her pockets.

Did you love him? he asked her. Yes, she had loved him, wanted to love him. She had not known about his English girlfriend. After the honeymoon, when he brought her to Edinburgh and started acting strange, she asked him and he told her everything.

Would you believe it, she said, his family now blame me for the divorce? They say I wasn't clever enough, I didn't try hard enough. They're going around Khartoum saying all these things about me. That's why I don't want to go back. But I'll have to eventually when my visa runs out.

I'm glad I'm not pregnant, she went on. I thank Allah every day that I didn't become pregnant.

After that they spoke about faith. He told her how he had become a Muslim. He spoke about his former chemistry teacher – after meeting again they had fallen back into the swing of their old teacher-student relationship. She listened, fascinated. She asked him questions. What was his religion before? He had been a Catholic. Has he always believed in God? Yes. Why on earth did he convert?

She seemed almost surprised by his answers. She associated Islam with her dark skin, her African blood, her own weakness. She couldn't really understand why anyone like him would want to join the wretched of the world. But he spoke with warmth. It made her look at him properly, as if for the first time. Your parents probably don't like it, she said, and your friends? They won't like you changing. She was candid in that way.

And she was right. He had lost one friend after a bitter, unnecessary argument; another withdrew. His parents struggled to hide their dismay. Ever since he had dropped out of medical school, they had feared for his well-being, fretted that he would get sucked up into unemployment, drugs, depression; the underworld that throbbed and dragged itself parallel to their active middle-class life. Only last week, their neighbours' son had hanged himself (drugs, of course, and days without showering). There was a secret plague that targeted young men.

Despite their misgiving about his conversion to Islam, his parents eventually had to admit that he looked well; he put on a bit of weight, got a raise at work. If only he would not talk about religion. They did not understand that side of him that was theoretical, intangible, belonging to the spiritual world. If only he would not mention religion then it would be easier to pretend that nothing had changed. He was confident enough to humour them. Elated that the questions he had once asked – what's it all for, what does it all mean, what's the point of going on? – the questions that had tilted the walls around him and nearly smothered him, were now valid. They were questions that had answers, answers that provoked other questions, that opened new doors, that urged him to look at things in another way; like holding a cube in his hand, turning it round and round, or like moving around a tall column and looking at it from the other side. How different it was and how the same.

When he took her to meet his parents, the afternoon was a huge success. We're going to get married, he said, and there was a kind of relief in his mother's eyes. It was easier for his parents to accept that he was in love with a Muslim girl than it was to accept that he was in love with Islam.

* * *

From the balcony of his hotel room, he looked out at the Nile. Sunshine so bright that he saw strands of shimmering light. Palm trees, boats, the river so blue. Would the water be cool, he wondered, or tepid? He felt sleepy. The phone rang and he went indoors again, sliding the tinted glass door behind him.

Her happy voice again. What were you doing, why aren't you asleep, everyone sleeps this time in the afternoon, it's siesta time, you must be exhausted. Did you remember to bring dollar bills – not sterling, not travellers' cheques? You mustn't eat at the hotel, it will be terribly expensive, you must eat only with us here at home. Yes, we'll pick you up later. You'll come for dinner, you'll meet my parents. Don't forget the gifts. Are you going to dream of me?

He dreamt that he was still on the airplane. He woke up an hour later thirsty, looked up and saw a small arrow painted on the ceiling of the room. What was the arrow for? Out on the balcony, the contrast startled him. Sunset had softened the sky, rimmed the west with pinks and soft orange. The Nile was benign, the sky already revealing a few stars, the air fresher. Birds swooped and zigzagged.

He heard the *azan*; the first time in his life to hear it outdoors. It was not as spectacular as he had thought it would be, not as sudden. It seemed to blend with the sound of the birds and the changing sky. He started to figure out the direction of Mecca using the setting sun as his guide. Straight east or even a little to the north-east it would be now, not south-east like from Scotland. He located the east and when he went back into the room, understood the purpose of the arrow that was painted on the ceiling. The arrow was to show the hotel guests which way to face Mecca. After he prayed he went downstairs and looked for the swimming pool. He swam in water that was warm and pungent with chlorine. Twilight was swift. In no time the sky turned a dark purple with sharp little stars. It was the first time he had swam under a night sky.

* * *

Her house was larger than he had imagined, shabbier. It was full of people – she had five brothers and sisters, several nephews and nieces, an uncle who resembled an older, smaller version of Morgan Freeman and an aunt who was asleep on a string bed in the corner of the room. The television blared. Her mother smiled at him and offered him sweets. Her father talked to him in careful, broken English. Everyone stared at him, curious, pleased. Only the brother looked bored, stretched out on another string bed staring at the ceiling.

So now you've seen my family, she said, naming her sisters, her nieces and nephews. The names swam in his head. He smiled and smiled until he strained the muscles in his face.

Now you've seen where I grew up, she said, as if they had cleared a hurdle. He realised for the first time, the things she'd never had: a desk of her own, a room of her own, her own cupboard, her own dressing table, her own mug, her own packet of biscuits. She had always lived as part of a group, part of her family. What was that like? He didn't know. He did not know her well enough. He had yet to see her hair, he had yet to know what she looked like when she cried and what she looked like when she woke up in the morning.

She spoke after they had finished dinner. My uncle knows an English song. She was laughing again, sitting on the arm of the sofa. He wants to sing it for you.

Morgan Freeman's look-alike sat up straight in his armchair and sang, Cricket, lovely cricket at Lords where I saw it. Cricket, lovely cricket at Lords where I saw it.

Everyone laughed. After singing, the uncle was out of breath.

* * *

They went on outings which she organised. They went on a boat trip, a picnic in the forest, they visited the camel market. In each of these outings, they were accompanied by her brother, her sisters, her nephews and nieces, her girlfriends. They were never alone. He remembered Michael in *The Godfather*, climbing the hills of Italy with his fiancée and the unforgettable soundtrack, surrounded by armed guards and her numerous relatives. It was like that but without the guns. And instead of rolling hills, there was flat scrubland, the edges of a desert. He watched her, how she carried a nephew, how she smiled, how she unpeeled a grapefruit and gave him a piece to eat, how she giggled with her girlfriends. He took lots of photographs. She gave him strange fruit to eat. One was called *doum* and it was brown, large as an orange, almost hard as rock, with a woody taste and a straw-like texture. Only the thin outer layer was to be gnawed at and chewed, most of it was the stone. Another fruit was called *gongoleez*, sour, tangy, white chunks, chalky in texture to suck on and throw the black stones away. Tamarind to drink, *kerkadah* to drink, *turmus, kebkebeh, nabaq.* Peanut salad, stuffed aubergines, *moulah, kisra, waikah, mouloukhia.* Dishes he had eaten before in the Nile Café, dishes that were new. She never tired of saying to him, here, taste this, it's nice, try this.

Can't we be alone, just for a bit?

My family are very strict, especially because I'm divorced, they're very strict, she said, but her eyes were smiling.

Try and sort something out.

Next week after the wedding, you'll see me every day and get tired of me.

You know I can't ever get tired of you.

How can I know that?

She could flirt for hours given the chance. Now there was no chance because it was not clear whether her uncle, eyes closed and head nodding forward, was dozing in his armchair or eavesdropping.

* * *

Mid-morning in Ghamhouriah Street, after they had bought ebony to take back to his parents, he felt a tug on his shoulder, turned and found his rucksack slashed open, his passport missing. His camera too. He started to shout. Calm down, she said but he could not calm down. It was not only anger – there was plenty of that – but the eruption of latent fears, the slap of a nightmare. Her brother had parked the car in a bit of shade in a side street. They reached it now, her brother tenser than ever, she downcast and he clutching his ravaged rucksack. He kicked the tyre of the car, f- this and f- that. Furious, he was, and out to abuse the place, the time, the crime. The whole street stood still and watched a foreigner go berserk, as if they were watching a scene in an American movie. A car drove past and the driver craned his neck to get a better look, laughed. Please, she said, stop it, you're embarrassing me. He did not hear her. Her voice could not compete with the roar of anger in his ears.

We'll have to go to the British Embassy and get him a new passport, she said to her brother.

No, we'll have to go the police station and report this first. Her brother got in the car, wiped the sweat on his forehead with his sleeves.

Get in the car, she said to him. We'll have to go to the police station and report your stolen passport.

He got in the car, fuming.

The police station was surprisingly pleasant. It was shady, cool. A bungalow and several outbuildings. They were treated well, given cold water, tea. He refused to drink the tea, sat in a sulk. Do you know how much that camera cost, he hissed, and it's not insured?

She shrugged, less shocked by what had happened than he was. Soothed by the drink, she started to tease him. They'll chop off the hand of the thief who stole your camera. Really, they will. Her brother laughed with her.

I really can't see what's so funny.

Can't you take a joke? she said and there was an edge to her voice. Afterwards they drove in silence to the British Embassy. There, they endured a long queue.

The Embassy staff hummed and hawed. They did not like to hear of passports getting stolen. And as one question led to another they were not overjoyed either to hear of people getting married in a few days' time. They interrogated her and her brother, broad, flat questions but still she felt sullied and small.

Coming out of the embassy, she was anything but calm. What did they think, what were they trying to insinuate – that I stole your passport, as if I am desperate to go back there?

What's that supposed to mean?

It's supposed to mean what it means. You think you're doing me a big favour by marrying me?

No, I don't think that, of course not ...

They do. They do, the way they were talking. Sneering at me and you didn't even notice!

Okay, okay, calm down.

A small boy touched his arm, begging. Gnarled fist, black skin turned grey from malnutrition, one eye clogged with thick mucus. He flinched at the unpleasant touch, felt guilty, fumbled in his pockets and started to take out a 200-dinar note.

Are you out of your mind, she said, giving him that amount? He'll get mugged for it. She opened her bag and gave the boy instead some coins and an orange.

As she got in the car, she told her brother about the beggar and they both laughed in a mocking way. Laughing at him in Arabic, the height of rudeness.

Perhaps you can contribute to the petrol then, the brother drawled, given you have so much cash to spare. I've burnt a lot of gas chauffeuring you and your fiancée around, you know.

Right, if this is what you want. He yanked out the notes from his wallet and slammed them down near the handbrake.

Thanks, her brother said, but when he picked up the wad of cash, he stared at it like it was not much, like he had expected more.

She sighed and looked out of the window. It was as if the theft had brought out all the badness in them.

He thought of saying, drop me at the hotel. He thought of giving up and leaving for Scotland the next day. That would punish her for laughing at him, that would hurt her. But he did not ask to be dropped off. He did not give up. True, he had no passport and would not be able to travel, but something else made him stay.

They walked into disarray. Her house, almost unrecognisable for the sheer number of people who were distraught, in shock. A woman was pushing the furniture to one side, another dropped a mattress on the floor; everywhere weeping, weeping and a few hoarse voices shouting orders. Her uncle, Morgan Freeman, had died, dozing in his armchair.

For a moment, the three of them stood in the middle of the room, frozen in disbelief. The brother started to ask questions in a loud voice.

That's it, she hissed, we'll never have our wedding now, not in the middle of this mourning, never, never. And she burst into tears.

Before he could respond, her brother led him away, saying the house would be for the women now, we have to go outside. Come on.

The garden was hell that time of day, sun scorching the grass, reflecting on the concrete slabs of the garage. How precious shade was in this part of the world, how quickly a quarrel could be pushed aside, how quickly the dead were taken to their graves. Where was he now, the uncle who sang Cricket, lovely cricket? Somewhere indoors being washed with soap, perfumed and then wrapped in white; that was the end then, without preliminaries. He could faint standing in the sun like this, without a passport, without her, without the reassurance that their wedding would go ahead. It couldn't be true. But it was, and minute after minute passed with him standing in the garden. Where was her brother now, who had previously watched his every move while she had circled him with attention, advice, plans? She was indoors, sucked up in rituals of grief he knew nothing about. Well, he could leave now, slip away unnoticed. He could walk to the main road and hail a taxi – something he had not done before because she and her brother had picked him up and dropped him back at the hotel every single day. Death, the destroyer of pleasures.

The body was being taken away. There it was shrouded in white and the shock of seeing that face again, asleep, fast asleep. The folds of nostrils and lips, the pleasing contrast of white hair against dark skin. He found himself following her brother into the car, getting into what now had become his seat at the back, two men crammed in next to him, an elderly man sat in front. The short drive to the mosque, rows of men. He had prayed that special prayer for the dead once before in Edinburgh – for a still-born baby. It did not involve any kneeling, was brief, cool. Here it was also raw, the fans whirling down from the ceiling, the smell of sweat and haste.

They drove out of town to the cemetery. He no longer asked himself why he was accompanying them, it seemed the right thing to do. In the car, there was a new ease between them, a kind of bonding because they had prayed together. They began to talk of the funeral announcement that went out on the radio after the news, the obituaries that would be published in the newspaper the next day. He half-listened to the Arabic he could not understand, to the summary in English which one of them would suddenly give, remembering his presence.

Sandy wind blowing, a home that was flat ground, a home that had no walls, no doors. My family's cemetery, her brother said suddenly, addressing him. Once he married her and took her back with him to Edinburgh would he be expected to bring her back here if God forbid, she died? Why think these miserable thoughts? A hole was eventually made in the ground, you would think they were enjoying the scooping out of dirt, so wholeheartedly were they digging. With the sleeve of his shirt, he wiped the sweat off his brow – he was beginning to act like them – since when did he wipe his face with his shirtsleeves in Edinburgh? He wanted a glass of cold water but they were lowering the uncle in the grave now. They put him in a niche, wedged him in so that when they filled the grave, the soil they poured in did not fall on him.

For the next three days, he sat in the tent that had been set up in the garden for the men. A kind of normality prevailed, people pouring in to pay their condolences, the women going indoors, the men to the tent. A flow of water glasses, coffee, tea, the buzz of flies. Rows of metal chairs became loose circles and knots, as old friends caught up with each other, a laugh here and there could be heard. What's going to happen to your wedding now? he was asked. He shrugged – he did not want to talk about it, was numbed by what had happened, dulled by the separation from her that the mourning customs seemed to impose. In the tent, the men agreed that the deceased had had a good death; no hospital, no pain, no Intensive Care and he was in his eighties, for God's sake, what more do you expect? A strange comfort in that tent. He fell into this new routine. After breakfast in the hotel, he would walk along the Nile, after passing the Presidential Palace, wave down a taxi, go to her house. He never met her and she never phoned him. After spending the day in the tent and having lunch with her brother and his friends, one of them would offer him a lift back to the Hilton. Late in the evening or the early morning, he would go swimming. Every day he could hold his breath underwater longer. When he went for a walk, he saw army trucks carrying young soldiers in green uniforms. The civil war in the south had gone on for years and wasn't drawing to an end – on the local TV station there were patriotic songs, marches. He had thought, from the books he'd read and the particular British Islam he had been exposed to, that in a Muslim country he would find elegance and reason. Instead he found melancholy, a sensuous place, life stripped to the bare bones.

On the third evening after the funeral, the tent was pulled down; the official mourning period was over.

I want to talk to you, he said to her brother, perhaps we could go for a walk.

They walked in a street calmed by the impending sunset. Only a few cars passed. He said, I can't stay here for long. I have to go back to my work in Scotland.

I'm sorry, the brother said, we could not have your wedding.

But you understand …

It's going to be difficult for me to come again. I think we should go ahead with our plans …

We can't celebrate at a time like this.

It doesn't have to be a big celebration.

You know, she had a big wedding party last time?

No, I didn't know. She didn't tell me.

I blame myself, her brother suddenly blurted out, that son of a dog and what he did to her. I knew, you see, I heard rumours that he was going with that girl but I didn't think much of it, I thought it was just a fling he was having and he'd put his girlfriend away once he got married.

They walked in silence after that, the sound of their footsteps on crumbling asphalt. There was movement and voices in the houses around them, the rustle and barks of stray dogs.

Finally her brother said, I suppose we could have the marriage ceremony at my flat. But just the ceremony, no party …

No, no, there's no need for a party …

I'll talk to my father and my mother, see if they approve of the idea.

Yes, please, and after the ceremony … ?

After the ceremony you can take her back with you to your hotel …

Right.

Her father has to agree first.

Yes, of course.

He walked lighter now, but there was still another hitch.

You know, her brother said, we lost a lot of money marrying her off to that son of a dog. A lot of money. And now again this time … even just for a simple ceremony at my place, I will have to buy drinks, sweets, pay for this and that.

On a street corner, money was exchanged between them. He handed her brother one fifty-dollar bill after the other, not stopping until he sensed a saturation.

Thanks, better not tell her about this, okay? My sister's always been sensitive and she doesn't realise how much things cost.

His hand trembled a little as he put his wallet away. He had previously paid a dowry (a modest one, the amount decided by her) and he had brought the gifts in good faith. Now he felt humiliated, as if had been hoodwinked or as if he had been so insensitive as to underestimate his share in the costs. Or as if he had paid for her.

***

On the night before the wedding, he slept lightly, on and off, so the night seemed to him elongated, obtuse. At one time he dreamt of a vivid but unclear sadness and when he woke he wished that his parents were with him, wished that he was not alone, getting married all alone. Where were the stag night, the church wedding, invitation cards, a reception and speeches? His older brother had got married in church wearing the family kilt. It had been a sunny day and his mother had worn a blue hat. He remembered the unexpected sunshine, the photos. He had turned his back on these customs, returned them as if they were borrowed, not his. He had no regrets, but he had passed the stage of rejection now, burnt out the zeal of the new convert, was less proud, more ready to admit to himself what he missed. No, his parents could not have accompanied him. They were not hardy enough to cope with the heat, the mosquitoes, the maimed beggars in the street, all the harshness that even a good hotel could not shield. Leave them be, thank them now humbly in the dark for the generous cheque they had given him.

He dreamt he was being chased by the man who had ripped his rucksack, robbed his passport and camera. He woke up sweaty and thirsty. It was three in the morning, not yet dawn. He prayed, willing himself to concentrate, to focus on what he was saying, who he was saying it to. In this late hour of the night, before the stir of dawn, all was still even his mind, which usually buzzed with activity, even his feelings, which tumbled young. Just a precious stillness, patience, patience for the door to open, for the contact to be made, for the comforting closeness. He had heard a talk once at the mosque, that there are certain times of the day and the year when Allah answers prayers indiscriminately, fully, immediately – so, who knows, you might one moment pray and be spot-on, you might ask and immediately be given.

After dawn he slept and felt warm as if he had a fever. But he felt better when he woke late with the phone ringing and her clear voice saying, I'm so excited I'm going to be coming to the Hilton to stay with you. I've never stayed in a Hilton before, I can't wait.

It was a matter of hours now.

* * *

Her brother's flat was in a newly built area, a little deserted, out of the way. One of her cousins had picked him up from the hotel and now they both shuffled up the stairs. The staircase was in sand, not yet laid out in tiles or concrete; there was a sharp smell of paint and bareness. The flat itself was neat and simple, a few potted plants, a large photograph of the Ka'ba. The men; her brother, father, various relations and neighbours whom he recognised from the days in the mourning tent, occupied the front room, the one near the door. The women were at the back of the flat. He couldn't see them, couldn't see her.

Shaking hands, the hum of a general conversation in another language. The imam wore a white jellabiya, a brown cloak, a large turban. He led them for the Maghrib prayer and after that the ceremony began. Only it was not much of a ceremony, but a signing of a contract between the groom and the bride's father. The imam pushed away the dish of dates that was on the coffee table and started to fill out a form. The date in the western calendar, the date in the Islamic calendar. The amount of dowry (the original figure she had named and not the additional dollars her brother had taken on the street corner). The name of the bride. The name of her father who was representing her. The name of the groom who was representing himself.

But that is not a Muslim name. The imam put the pen down, sat back in his chair.

Show him your certificate from the mosque in Edinburgh, urged her brother, the one you showed me when you first arrived.

I can't, he said, it was stolen or it fell out when the things in my bag were stolen.

No matter, the brother sighed and turned to speak to the imam. He's a Muslim for sure. He prayed with us. Didn't you see him praying just now behind you?

Did they tell you I have eyes at the back of my head? Laughter ... that didn't last long.

Come on sheikh, one of the guests said, we're all gathered here for this marriage to take place *inshallah*. We've all seen this foreigner praying, not just now but also on the days of the funeral. Let's not start to make problems.

Look, he will recite for you the Fatiha, the brother said, won't you? He put his hand on his shoulder as a way of encouragement. Come on sheikh, another guest said, these people aren't even celebrating or having a party. They're in difficult circumstances, don't make things more difficult. The bride's brother said he saw an official certificate, that should be enough.

Inshallah there won't be any difficulties, someone ventured. Let him recite, the imam said, looking away.

He was sweating now. No, not everyone's eyes were on him, some were looking away, hiding their amusement or feeling embarrassed on his behalf. He sat forward, his elbows on his knees.

In the Name of Allah, the Compassionate, the Merciful, her brother whispered helpfully.

In the Name of Allah, the Compassionate, the Merciful, he repeated, his voice hoarse but loud enough. All praise to Allah, Lord of the Worlds and the rest followed, one stammered letter after the other, one hesitant word after the other.

Silence, the scratch of a pen. His hand in her father's hand. The *Fatiha* again, everyone saying it to themselves, mumbling it fast, raising their palms, *Ameen*, wiping their faces.

Congratulations, we've given her to you now. She's all yours now.

* * *

When he saw her, when he walked down the corridor to where the women were gathered, when the door opened for him and he saw her, he could only say, oh my God, I can't believe it! It was as if it was her and not her at the same time. Her familiar voice saying his name. Those dark slanting eye smiling at him. But her hair long and falling on her shoulders (she had had it chemically relaxed), make-up that made her glow, a secret glamour. Her dress in soft red, sleeveless, she was not thin ...

God, I can't believe it! And the few people around them laughed. A haze in the room, smoke from the incense they were burning, the perfume making him light-headed, tilting his mind, a dreaminess in the material of her dress, how altered she was, how so much more of her there was. He coughed.

Is the incense bothering you?

A blur as someone suggested that the two of them sit out on the balcony. It would be cooler there, just for a while, until they could get a lift to the hotel. He followed her out into a sultry darkness, a privacy granted without doors or curtains, the classic African sky dwarfing the city below.

She did not chat like she usually did. He could not stop staring at her and she became shy, overcome. He wanted to tell her she was beautiful, he wanted to tell her about the ceremony, about the last few days and how he had missed her, but the words, any words, wouldn't come. He was stilled, choked by a kind of brightness.

At last she said, Can you see the henna pattern on my palms? It's light enough.

He could trace, in the grey light of the stars, delicate leaves and swirls.

I'll wear gloves, she said, when we go back to Scotland, I'll wear gloves, so as not to shock everyone.

No, you needn't do that, he said, it's lovely.

It was his voice that made her ask. Are you all right, you're not well? She put her hand on his cheek, on his forehead. So that was how soft she was, so that was how she smelt, that was her secret. He said, without thinking, it's been rough for me, these past days. Please, feel sorry for me.

I do, she whispered, I do.

Farida's Eyes

It started with the writing on the blackboard becoming hazy and crumbly, eventually just a tangle of white threads. The questions in the history test should have been clear and familiar but Farida couldn't read them. And if she couldn't read them, how could she answer them? She would get a zero. She had never got a zero before.

Farida learned like she breathed, without ceremony, without effort. Information entered her mind with ease and she picked up skills with grace and gratitude. Her homework was completed on time, her exercise books were spotless and she never ever forgot a textbook at home. As a result, her teachers were satisfied, her mother was pleased and though her father never voiced his approval, he grudgingly paid the school fees on time.

Farida blinked and, just before her eyes closed, some of

the words on the blackboard momentarily came into focus. What had looked like 'cement' became 'crescent'; what had looked like 'umbrella' became 'utensils.' She craned her neck forward and narrowed her eyes. They started to water, which blurred her vision even more. Now 'utensils' deteriorated to 'elcmiebs' and the rest of the words were just one block after the other of padded, twisted chalk. Even the question numbers, predictably placed at the beginning of each line and the question marks at the end, merged with the rest of the words. There was only the steady forward slope of the cursive; 'y' and 'g' were indistinguishable, while capital 'M' and capital 'T' stood out clearly. Within the words, the vowels gummed together, 'c' could very well be 'e', and 'n', 'r', and 'm' blurred into the same wriggle. Dots sprinkled high pointed to the obvious but that was not much help. Her classmates were busy writing while Sister Carlotta walked between the rows of desks, ruler in hand, making sure that no girls were whispering or holding their textbooks open on their laps.

'Sister Carlotta,' Farida whispered when the nun passed by. 'Can I move to the front of the class to see the blackboard better?' Because Farida was tall, she had to sit at the back of the class so as not to block the blackboard for the other girls. She did not like sitting at the back. The studious girls always sat in the front rows, attentive and close to the teacher. Farida's neighbours were those girls who were either slow learners or bored with school. They would giggle together, pass notes and even doze on hot days. Farida resented that her height forced her to be in their company.

Sister Carlotta put her hands on her waist. 'Didn't I tell you that you have to go to the doctor and get yourself fitted for glasses?' Her own thick, heavy-framed pair slid down her skinny nose. The lenses were convex pools, blowing her eyes up to the size of an owl's. 'Did you tell your father?'

Farida did not want to be questioned now. She wanted to know what was written on the board. She wanted to write down the answers. She had the material memorised and it was bristling in her head, jostling to spill over on to the page. 'My father said no need.' She felt ashamed.

Sister Carlotta gave an exasperated sigh and slapped her sturdy arms against her white skirt. The ruler scraped against the stiff cotton. 'Nonsense, nonsense! When will these people learn? Come and sit in front then. But there are no vacant benches today. Oh, just sit at my desk.'

It was strange to sit at the teacher's desk, up on the podium. Farida felt a sense of awe and privilege. There was a strong smell of chalk and her classmates sat several feet below, rows and rows of girls in their navy-blue uniform. It occurred to Farida for the first time that she wanted to be a teacher when she grew up. But this was not a time for daydreams. Already she had lost five minutes. She had to make haste. The questions were clear now in Sister Carlotta's rounded cursive. Five questions each carrying twenty points, and Farida knew the answers to them all.

* * *

At home she lay awake and listened to her parents talking. 'She will fail school,' her mother was saying. 'Without a pair of glasses she will not be able to read. This is what her teacher said.'

Her father's voice was louder. 'More expenses. Not just the fees, the uniform, the books – now you come up with something new. She will look ugly in glasses!'

Farida did not want to look ugly either. How many girls at school wore glasses? A handful, and they were mocked by everyone else. When they took off their glasses, there were dark shadows under their eyes, wedges on their noses from the pressure of the frames. Their short-sighted eyes looked vacant and strange. As for Sister Carlotta, her eyes behind her glasses were almost frightening with their dark, animal hugeness, and how the left was slightly larger than the right, the right more heavy-lidded. The convex thickness of the lens looked like rings within rings. It reminded Farida of throwing a stone in a pond and watching the ripples spread out. On Sister Carlotta's glasses, the ripples were fixed and almost eerie. It made talking to her awkward because while Farida knew that Sister Carlotta was seeing her, it was tricky to make contact with the fluid, overblown eyes in their deep pools of glass.

In their literature class, Sister Carlotta read to them from *Flowers for Mrs Harris*. Mrs Harris was a comic figure, a charlady flying to Paris to buy a Dior dress. There was a picture of her on the cover of the book, a sharp elderly lady with white hair tied in a bun. 'My mother,' said

Sister Carlotta with a smile, 'is exactly like Mrs Harris.'
The class roared with laughter. Sister Carlotta was the best
teacher they had, the only one who never brought down
her ruler on their palms and knuckles. When Farida asked
if her mother also liked designer dresses, Sister Carlotta
did not find her impertinent. Instead she explained that
her mother now had macular degeneration and that
unlike Mrs Harris, she could not see much through a
shop window. In the library, Farida read up on 'macular
degeneration'. She imagined darkness in the middle and
blurred sight on the periphery of her vision. Would you
have to twist your head to read? It would be like forever
watching an eclipse, the round black centre and rays of
light slithering on the side.

Sister Carlotta began to allow Farida to sit at the front
of the class despite the rule that tall girls must sit at the
back. The other teachers were not as kind. Some of them
did not believe that Farida was short-sighted; some of them
did not care. So Farida's grades started to slip. Lessons
became boring because she could only understand bits of
them. Science made no sense without clear diagrams and
mistaking a plus sign for a multiplication sign in Maths
lessons meant the answer was completely wrong.

'Your semester report card is very bad,' scolded her
mother as she picked up the new baby. 'You have failed
every subject except History and Literature!'

'Because Sister Carlotta teaches ...'

Her father interrupted, 'You will be held back a year if

you don't improve. Why have you become so lazy?'

Farida did not know how to reply.

'Maybe it's her eyesight,' said Mama. 'Maybe she does need these glasses.' She did not sound convinced.

'Don't make excuses for her. Your daughter has turned stupid.'

* * *

Farida felt stupid. She was no longer one of the clever pupils. She even made friends with the girls who didn't care about school, the ones who sat next to her in the back row. She chatted during lessons, hummed tunes. When she was reprimanded, she laughed it off pretending not to care. Ten stinging swipes of the ruler from the Maths teacher had her licking and blowing her palms. The blackboard became a fuzzy, distant place, neither clear nor interesting

She could not see the expression on Sister Carlotta's face, but something in the way she held herself made Farida pay attention. Sister Carlotta's voice sounded strained and high-pitched. 'I am going away, back to Rome. I have to. My mother ... remember I told you she resembled Mrs Harris? She died last night.'

At the mention of Mrs Harris, most of the girls burst out laughing. Sister Carlotta's face turned red. Even Farida could see the change in colour. 'How dare you laugh!' she screeched. Her eyes darted in seemingly opposite directions; they bulged as if she did not have any eyelids. 'I tell you that my mother died and you laugh!' She sounded like she was going to cry.

The laughter died down. Farida wanted Sister Carlotta to know that she hadn't laughed like the other silly girls. She strained to see if Sister Carlotta was looking in her direction but could not be sure. It was time to ask permission to move to the front rows, to remind Sister Carlotta of her eyes – but today Farida felt shy, and today Sister Carlotta was too preoccupied to remember.

In the following weeks a substitute teacher who was very mindful of the seating rules came in, and Farida's grades slipped in History and Literature too. She was now heading for the ultimate humiliation, repeating the grade. Her classmates would go forward and she would be held back. She would be surrounded by girls younger than her. Farida, already tall for her age, would be a giant among them. The glasses? No one spoke about them at home now. There were other urgent matters: how her older brother got into trouble with the police, her baby brother's fever, a quarrel between her mother and the neighbour, the rise in the price of sugar, an uncle coming to visit. No one had time for Farida's eyes.

In the middle of the night, in the pitch darkness without moon or stars, a thought entered Farida's mind and made her cold with fear. What if her eyesight kept getting worse? What if she became completely blind? She would be groping in the dark – no school, no books, no cinema. Just voices and sounds.

One day, running to open the door for the milkman, she accidentally knocked down a glass of water that her father had left on the floor. 'Are you blind?' he shouted. 'Clean up this mess.' She did, while he fetched in the milk. There were big, jagged pieces of glass and many tiny splinters spread across the soaking floor. She picked them up one by one, peering to make sure that she didn't miss any. Are you blind? Tears rose to her eyes and when she sobbed, they became red and itchy. Her head ached and she felt that her vision was even worse than before.

In the middle of the night she could not find the bathroom. Her knees knocked against the bed as she ran her palms along the wall. Wall and flat wall which should give way to a corner, a corridor and then the little toilet with a window and the grey necessary chink of starlight, but her fingers just found wall and more wall. Even the light switch, though she would get into trouble for waking her baby brother, seemed to have been swallowed up by flatness. Had blindness arrived? Was this what it was like? The pressure on her bladder and the need for help. She pressed her knees together and, just as she was about to wet her pants, cried out loud for her mother.

The next day she stayed home from school. She tied a hair ribbon around her eyes and started to write in her exercise book. She wrote, 'I want to be a teacher when I grow up,' and wondered if she had reached the edge of the page, if she needed now to move her hand back to the starting margin. There was no way of knowing. It made no difference if she looked down at the copybook or straight up, it was the same pressure of the ribbon on her closed eyes. She had to guess and keep on writing. When she lifted up the ribbon, she was surprised to see that her writing was no longer in straight lines; the words were no longer flat adjacent to each other. Instead they curved up and down, in the shape of hills. The words were clear but, without being able to see the margins or the ruled page, the sentences had strange circular shapes, cramped because she had been too cautious in her estimation of the margins. She covered her eyes again and groped her way around the house, practicing. She made her bed and helped her mother in the kitchen. At first her mother laughed but when Farida spilled the lentils on the floor, she shooed her out of the kitchen. 'Can we get a dog?' Farida asked.

She would sit with her back to the television, kissing her photos goodbye. Bruises covered her knees and forehead from stumbling unsuccessfully around the house. Then her exasperated father would snatch away the ribbon and she would be exposed to the sudden glare of sunlight and shapes, movements and colours. And still, she went on practicing.

* * *

One day there was a knock at the door. Sister Carlotta stood in the doorway. She looked exactly the same with her white habit, long skirt and the large cross hung around her neck. Farida had never seen those huge eyes outside of school before. Sister Carlotta was back in town; she had not stayed in Rome forever.

'Who is it?' her mother's voice called out.

Farida couldn't reply.

Sister Carlotta smiled, 'Tell your parents that I am here to talk about your eyes.'

Afterwards, Farida would remember glimpses of that visit like a series of photographs placed one after the other. Her mother's anxious face, the way she fussed over this most unexpected of guests. Her father, woken hastily from his siesta, bewildered and resentful yet as bashful as a boy; Sister Carlotta holding the baby in her arms. Her firm, calm voice, 'I came here today to talk about Farida's eyes.'

How did she convince Farida's parents? She explained, she coaxed, she threatened that they would earn the reputation of being miserly and negligent. And they took heed because she was European and they were not, because she was educated and they were not, because she was a nun and had authority, because she was a teacher. And most importantly, because she spoke the truth. She scolded them. She shamed them. And she reasoned too. How much money did the good man spend on cigarettes? Didn't they know of the free health clinic? That was where they could go to get cheap frames.

The next morning Farida and her mother went to the clinic. It was crowded and they had to wait for hours, during which Farida squirmed with boredom and her baby brother cried. Finally inside, the doctor's room was cool. He was smiling and wearing a clean coat. Farida had to sit on a special chair; one eye was covered and she was asked to look at figures on a screen. They were rows of the letter 'C' sometimes upside down, backwards or facing up. The doctor explained that he wanted her to say which way the 'C' was facing. How easy it was! Farida sailed through the first lines but she started to falter as the 'C's' got smaller. The doctor fitted round frames over her eyes and slid different lenses in the frames, sometimes on top of each other. They made a *shlick*, *shlick* noise. The tiny 'C's' on the bottom row became sharp and distinct. A lens for her right eye, a lens for her left eye. Everyone, the doctor explained, needed a special prescription. He smelt nice, he was clever and he cared about her eyes. Farida decided she had changed her mind and wanted to be a doctor when she grew up.

On the first day she wore her glasses to school, the frames felt heavy on her face. She imagined that all the girls were staring at her but only a few reacted. One of them said, 'Congratulations.' Another covered her mouth with her hand and giggled, another screeched in surprise – but only one girl said she looked ugly.

Souvenirs

They set out early, before sunset. Not the right time for visiting, but it was going to be a long drive and his sister Manaal said she would not be able to recognise the painter's house in the dark. The car slipped from the shaded carport into the white sunlight of the afternoon, the streets were empty, their silence reminiscent of dawn.

Since he had come on the plane from Scotland two weeks ago, Yassir had not gone out at this time of day. Instead he had rested after lunch wearing his old jellabiya. He would lie on one of the beds that were against the walls of the sitting room, playing with a toothpick in his mouth and talking to Manaal without looking at her. On the bed perpendicular to his, she would lie with her feet near his head so that, had they been children, she might have reached out and pulled his hair with her toes. And the child Yassir would have let his heels graze the white wall leaving brown stains for which he would be punished later. Now they talked slowly, probing for common interests and remembering things past, gossiping lightly about others, while all the time the air cooler blew the edges of the bedsheets just a little, intermittently, and the smells of lunch receded. Then the air cooler's sound would take over, dominate the room, blowing their thoughts away and they would sleep until the time came when all the garden was in shade.

In this respect, Yassir had slotted easily into the life of Khartoum, after five years on the North Sea oil rigs, noisy helicopter flights to and from Dyce airport, a grey sea with waves as turbulent as the sky. Five years of two weeks offshore, two weeks on with Emma in Aberdeen. No naps after lunch there and yet here he could lie and know that the rhythms the air cooler whispered into his heart were familiar, well-known. When he had first arrived he had put fresh straw into the air cooler's box. Standing outdoors on an upturned Pepsi crate, he had wedged open the grimy perforated frame with a screwdriver, unleashed cobwebs and plenty of dust; fresh powdery dust and solid fluffs that had lost all resemblance to sand. The old bale of straw had shrunk over the years, gone dark and rigid from the constant exposure to water. He oiled the water pump and put in the new bale of straw. Its smell filled the house for days, the air that blew out was cooler. For this his mother had thanked him and like other times before, prayed that he would only find good people in his path. It was true, he was always fortunate in the connections he made, in the people who held the ability to further his interests. In the past teachers, now his boss, his colleagues, Emma.

But, 'Your wife – what's her name?' was how his mother referred to Emma. She would not say Emma's name. She would not 'remember' it. It would have been the same if Emma had been Jane, Alison or Susan, any woman from 'outside'. Outside that large pool of names his mother knew and could relate to. That was his punishment – nothing more, nothing less. He accepted it as the nomad bears the times of drought which come to starve his cattle, biding time, waiting for the tightness to run its course and the rain that must eventually fall. Manaal would smile in an embarrassed way when their mother said that. And as if time had dissolved the age gap between them, she would attempt a faint defence. 'Leave him alone, Mama,' she would say, in a whisper, avoiding their eyes, wary, lest her words instead of calming, provoked the much-feared outburst. Manaal had met Emma two years ago in Aberdeen. What she had told his mother about Emma, what she had said to try to drive away the rejection that gripped her, he didn't know.

For Yassir, Emma was Aberdeen. Unbroken land after the sea. Real life after the straight lines of the oil rig. A kind of freedom. Before Emma, his leave onshore had floated, never living up to his expectations. And it was essential for those who worked on the rigs that those onshore days were fulfilling enough to justify the hardship of the rigs. A certain formula was needed, a certain balance which evaded him. Until one day he visited the dentist for two fillings and, with lips frozen with procaine, read out loud the name, Emma, written in Arabic, on a golden necklace that hung around the receptionist's throat.

'Your wife – what's her name?' his mother said, as if clumsily smudging out a fact, hurting it. A fact, a history: three years ago he drove Emma to the maternity ward in Foresterhill, in the middle of a summer's night that looked like twilight, to deliver a daughter who did not make her appearance until the afternoon of the following day. Samia changed in the two weeks that he did not see her. Her growth marked time like nothing else did. Two weeks offshore, two weeks with Emma and Samia, two weeks offshore again, Emma driving him to the heliport, the child in her own seat at the back. A fact, a history. Yet here, when Manaal's friends visited, some with toddlers, some with good jobs, careers, there was a 'see what you've missed' atmosphere around the house. An atmosphere that was neither jocular nor of regret. So that he had come to realise, with the sick bleakness that accompanies truth, that his mother imagined that he could just leave Emma and leave the child, come home, and those five years would have been just an aberration, time forgotten. He could marry one of Manaal's friends, one who would not mind that he had been married before, that he had left behind a child somewhere in Europe. A bride who would regard all that as a man's experience. When talking to her friends she would say the word 'experienced' in a certain way, smiling secretly.

* * *

Because the streets were silent, Yassir and Manaal were silent too, as if by talking they would disturb those who were resting indoors. Yassir drove slowly, pebbles spat out from under the wheels, he was careful to avoid the potholes. The open windows let in dust but closing them would be suffocating. From their house in Safia they crossed the bridge into Khartoum and it was busier there, more cars, more people walking in the streets. That part of the journey, the entry into Khartoum, reminded him of the Blue Nile Cinema, which was a little way under the bridge. He remembered as a student walking back from the cinema, late at night to the Barracks, as his hostel was called, because it was once an army barracks. He used to walk with his friends in a kind of swollen high, full of the film he had just seen. Films like *A Man for All Seasons*, *Educating Rita*, *Chariots of Fire*.

There was still a long way for them to go, past the Extension, beyond the airport, past Riyadh to the newly built areas of Taif and El-Ma'moura. Not a very practical idea, a drain of the week's ration of petrol and there was the possibility that the painter would not be in and the whole journey would have been wasted. Manaal was optimistic though. 'They'll be in,' she said, '*Inshallah*. Especially if we get there early enough before they go out anywhere.' There were no telephones in El-Ma'moura; it was a newly built area with no street numbers, no addresses.

That morning, he had mentioned buying a painting or two to take back to Aberdeen and Manaal had suggested Ronan K. He was English; his wife gave private English lessons (Manaal was once her student). Now in the car when he asked more about him she said, 'For years he sat doing nothing, he had no job, maybe he was painting. I didn't know about that until the Hilton commissioned him to do some paintings for the cafeteria. No one knows why this couple live here. They are either crazy or they are spies. Everyone thinks they are spies.'

'You all like to think these sensational things,' he said. 'What is there to spy on anyway?'

'They're nice though,' she said. 'I hope they are not spies.' Yassir shook his head, thinking it was hopeless to talk sense to her.

The paintings were not his idea, they were Emma's. Emma was good with ideas, new suggestions – it was one of the things he admired about her. Yassir didn't know much about painting. If he walked into a room he would not notice the paintings on the wall and he secretly thought they were an extravagance. But then he felt like that about many of the things Emma bought. What he considered luxuries, she considered necessities. Like the Bambi wallpaper in Samia's room must be bought to match the curtains, which match the bedspread, which match Thumper on the pillowcase. And there was a Bambi video, a Ladybird book, a pop-up book. He would grumble but she would persuade him. She would say that as a child she had cried in the cinema when Bambi's mother was shot. Popcorn could not stop the tears, the nasal flood.

This time Emma had asked, 'What can you get from Khartoum for the house?' They were eating muesli and watching television.

'Nothing. There's nothing there,' Yassir said.

'What do tourists get when they go there?'

'Tourists don't go there,' he said. 'It's not a touristy place. The only foreigners there are working.'

Once, when Yassir was in university, he had met a British journalist. The journalist was wearing shorts which looked comical because no one else wore shorts unless they were playing sports. He had chatted to Yassir and some of his friends.

'There must be something you can get,' Emma said. 'Things carved in wood, baskets ...'

'There's a shop which sells ivory things. Elephants made of ivory and things like that.'

'No. Not ivory.'

'I could get you a handbag made of crocodile skin?'

'No, yuck.'

'Snake skin?'

'Stop it, I'm serious.'

'Ostrich feathers?'

'No dead animals! Think of something else.'

'There's a bead market. Someone once told me about that. I don't know where it is though. I'll have to find out.'

'If you get me beads I can have them made here into a necklace.' Emma liked necklaces but not bracelets or earrings. The golden necklace with her name in Arabic was from an ex-boyfriend, a mud-logger who had been working rotational from the oil rigs in Oman.

'Change your mind and come with me. You can take the malaria pills, Samia can take the syrup and it's just a few vaccines ...'

'A few jabs! Typhoid, yellow fever, cholera, TB! And Samia might get bitten by this sandfly Manaal told us about when she came here. She is only three. It's not worth it – maybe when she's older ...'

'You're not curious to see where I grew up?'

'I am interested a bit but – I don't know – I've never heard anything good about that place.'

'This is just a two-week holiday, that's all. My mother will get to see you and Samia, you'll have a look around ...' he said, switching the television off.

'Paintings,' she said, 'that's what you should get. You can bring back paintings of all those things you think I should be curious about. Or just take lots of photographs and bring the beads.'

* * *

He bought the beads but did not take any photographs. He had shied away from that, as if unable to click a camera at his house, his old school, the cinemas that brought the sparkle of life abroad. So when Manaal said she knew this English painter, he was enthusiastic about the idea even though it was his last evening in Khartoum. Tomorrow his flight would leave for home. He hoped he would have with him some paintings for Emma. She would care about where each one went, on this wall or that. She cared about things more than he did. She even cared about Samia more than he did. Emma was in tune with the child's every burp and whimper. In comparison to Emma, Yassir's feelings for Samia were jammed up, unable to flow. Sometimes with the two of them he felt himself dispensable, he thought they could manage without him. They did just that when he was offshore. They had a life together: playgroup, kindergym, Duthie Park. When Manaal came to Aberdeen she said many times, 'Emma is so good with the child. She talks to her as if she is an adult.'

Yassir now wondered, as they drove down Airport Road, if Manaal had said such positive things to his mother. Or if she had only told of the first day of her visit to Aberdeen. The day she reached out to hold the sleeping child and Emma said, 'No, I'd rather you didn't. She'll be frightened if she wakes up and finds a stranger holding her.' The expression on Manaal's face had lingered throughout the whole visit as she cringed in Emma's jumpers that were too loose, too big for her. Then, as if lost in the cold, his sister hibernated, slept and slept through the nights and large parts of the days. So that Emma began to say, she must be ill, there must be something wrong with her, some disease, why does she sleep so much Yassir, why?

Possessive of Manaal, he had shrugged – Aberdeen's fresh air – and not explained that his sister had always been like that, easily tired, that she reacted to life's confusions by digging herself into sleep. When they left the airport behind them and began to pass Riyadh, Manaal suddenly said that to make sure they get to the right house, she had better drop in on her friend Zahra. Zahra's mother, a Bulgarian, was a good friend of Mrs K and would know where the house was.

'I thought you knew where it is?'

'I do, but it's better to be sure. It's on our way anyway.'

'Isn't it too early to go banging on people's doors?'

'No, it's nearly five. Anyway her parents are away – they've gone to Hajj.'

'Who? The Bulgarian woman? You're joking.'

'No, *wallahi*,' Manaal seemed amused by his surprise. 'Zahra's mother prays and fasts Ramadan. We were teasing her the last time I went there, telling her that when she comes back from Hajj, she'll start covering her hair and wearing long sleeves. And she said, 'No, never, your country is too hot; it's an oven.' Manaal did an impersonation of grammatically incorrect Arabic with a Bulgarian accent which made Yassir laugh. He thought of Zahra's father, a man who was able to draw his foreign wife to Islam, and Yassir attributed to him qualities of strength and confidence.

The house, in front of which Manaal told him to stop, had a high wall around it. The tops of the trees that grew inside fell over the wall shading the pavement. Manaal banged on the metal door – there was no bell. She banged with her palms, and peered through the chink in the door to see if anyone was coming.

Yassir opened the car door to let in some air but there was hardly any breeze. There were tears in the plastic of Manaal's seat from which bits of yellow foam protruded. There was a crack in the window, fine and long, like a map of the Nile and one of the doors in the back was stuck and could never be opened. This car, he thought, would not pass its MOT in Aberdeen; it would not be deemed 'roadworthy'. What keeps it going here is Baraka.

The car had seen finer days in his father's lifetime. Then it was solid and tinged with prestige. Now more than anything else, its decay was proof of the passing away of time, the years of Yassir's absence. He had suggested to his mother and Manaal that he should buy them a new one. Indeed this had been one of the many topics of his stay: a new car, the house needs fixing, parts of the garden wall are crumbling away, why don't you get out of this dump and move to a new house? But his mother and sister tended to put up with things. Like with Manaal recently losing her job. She had worked since graduation with a Danish aid agency, writing reports in their main office in

Souk Two. When they had reduced their operations in the South, staff cuts followed. 'Start looking for a new job,' he told her, 'or have you got certain plans that I don't know of yet?' She laughed and said, 'When you leave I'll start looking for a job and no, there are no certain plans. There is no one on the horizon yet.'

It was a joke between them. There is no one on the horizon yet. She wrote this at the bottom of letters, letters in Arabic that Emma could not read. Year after year. She was twenty-six now and he could feel the words touched by the frizzle of anxiety. 'Every university graduate is abroad, making money so that he can come back and marry a pretty girl like you,' he had said recently to her. 'Really?' she replied with a sarcasm that was not characteristic of her.

*** * ***

From the door of Zahra's house, Manaal looked at Yassir in the car and shrugged, then banged again with both hands. But she must have heard someone coming for she raised her hand to him and nodded.

The girl who opened the door had a towel wrapped around her hair like a turban. She kissed Manaal and he could hear, amidst their greetings, the words shower and sorry. They walked towards him, something he was not expecting and before he could get out of the car the girl leaned, and through the open window of the seat next to his, extended her hand. The car filled up with the smell of soap and shampoo, he thought his hand would later smell of her soap. She had the same colouring as his daughter Samia, the froth of cappuccino, dark-grey eyes, thick eyebrows. Her face was dotted with pink spots, round and raised like little sweets. He imagined those grey eyes soft with sadness when she examined her acne in the bathroom mirror, running her fingertips over the bumps.

With a twig and some pebbles, Zahra drew them a map of the painter's house in the dust of the pavement. She sat on her heels rather primly, careful not to get dust on her jellabiya. She marked the main road and where they should turn left. 'When you see a house with no garden walls, no fence,' she said, 'that's where you should turn left.'

She stood up, dusted off her hands and, when Manaal got into the car, she waved to them until they turned out of sight. Yassir drove back on to the main road, from the dust to the asphalt. The asphalt road was raised and because it had no pavements, its sides were continually being eroded, eaten away. They looked jagged, crumbly. The afternoon was beginning to mellow and sunset was drawing near.

'I imagine that when Samia grows up she will look like your friend,' he said.

'Maybe, yes. I haven't thought of it before,' Manaal said. 'Did you like the earrings for Samia?' He nodded. His mother had given him a pair of earrings for Samia. He had thanked her, not saying that his daughter's ears were not pierced.

'She's beginning to accept the situation.' His voice had a tinge of bravado about it. He was talking about his mother and Manaal knew. She was looking out of the window. She turned to him and said, 'She likes the photographs that you send. She shows them to everyone.'

Yassir had been sending photographs from Aberdeen. Photographs of Emma and Samia. Some were in the snow, some taken in the Winter Gardens at Duthie Park, some at home.

'So why doesn't she tell me that? Instead of 'What's her name?' or whatever she keeps saying?'

'You should have given her some idea very early on, you should have ... consulted her,' Manaal spoke slowly, with caution, like she was afraid.

'And what would she have said if I had asked her? Tell me, what do you think she would have said?'

'I don't know.'

'You do know.'

'How can I?'

'She would have said no and then what?'

'I don't know. I just know that it was wrong to suddenly write a letter and say "I got married" – in the past tense. Nobody does that.'

He didn't answer her. He did not like the hurt in her voice, like it was her own hurt and not their mother's.

As if his silence disturbed her she continued, 'It wasn't kind.'

'It was honest.'

'But it was hard. She was like someone ill when she read your letter. Defeated and ill ...'

'She'll come to accept it.'

'Of course she'll come to accept it. That's the whole point. It's inevitable but you could have made it easier for her, that's all.' Then in a lighter tone she said, 'Do something theatrical. Get down on your knees and beg for her forgiveness.'

They laughed at this together, somewhat deliberately to ease the tension. What he wanted to do was explain, speak about Emma and say: She welcomed me, I was on the periphery and she let me in. 'Do people get tortured to death in that dentist's chair or am I going to be the first?' he had asked Emma that day making her smile, when he stumbled out and spoke to her with lips numb with procaine.

'It would have been good if Emma and Samia had come with you,' Manaal was saying.

'I wanted that too.'

'Why didn't they?' She had asked that question before, as had others. He gave different reasons to different people. Now in the car he felt that Manaal was asking deliberately, wanting him to tell her the truth. Could he say that from this part of the world Emma wanted malleable pieces, not the random whole? She desired frankincense from the Body Shop, tahini safe in a supermarket container.

'She has fears,' he said.

'What fears?'

'I don't know. The sandfly, malaria ... Some rubbish like that.' He felt embarrassed and disloyal.

***

They heard the sunset *azan* when they began to look for the house without a garden wall, described by Zahra. But there were many houses like that; people built their homes and ran out of money by the time it came to build the garden wall. So they turned left off the asphalt road anyway when they reached El-Ma'moura, hoping that Manaal would be able to recognise the street or the house.

'Nothing looks familiar to you?' he asked.

'But everything looks different than the last time I was here,' she said. 'All those new houses, it's confusing.'

There were no roads and hardly any pavements, only tracks made by previous cars. They drove through dust and stones. The houses in various stages of construction stood in straight lines. In some parts, the houses formed a square around a large empty area, as if marking a place which would always be empty, where houses were not allowed to be built.

'Maybe it's this house,' Manaal said. He parked. They rang the bell but it was the wrong house.

Back in the car they drove through the different tracks and decided to ask around. How many foreigners were living in this area anyway? People were bound to know them.

Yassir asked a man sitting in front of his house, one

knee against his chest, picking his toenails. Near him an elderly man was praying, using a newspaper as a mat. The man didn't seem to know but he gave Yassir several elaborate suggestions.

Yassir asked some people who were walking past but again, they didn't know. This was taking a long time as everyone he asked seemed willing to engage him in conversation.

'It's your turn,' he said to Manaal when they saw a woman coming out of her house.

She went towards the woman and stood talking to her. Sunset was nearly over by then; the western sky, the houses, the dusty roads were all one colour. Like the flare that burns off the rig, he thought. Manaal stood, a dark silhouette against red and brick. One hand reached out to hold her hair from blowing and her thin elbows made an angle with her head and neck from which the light came through. This is what I would paint, Yassir thought, if I knew how. I would paint Manaal like this, with her elbows sticking out against the setting sun.

When she came back she seemed pleased. 'We're nearly there,' she said, 'that woman knew them. First right, and it's the second house.'

As soon as they turned right, Manaal recognised the one-storey house with the blue gate. She got out before him and rang the bell.

* * *

Ronan K. was older than Yassir had imagined. He looked like a football coach, overweight yet light in his movements. The light from the lamp near the gate made him look slightly bald. He recognised Manaal, and as they stepped into a large bare courtyard while he closed the gate behind them, she launched into a long explanation of why they had come and how they had nearly got lost on the way.

The house inside had no tiles on the floors – its surface was of uneven textured stone, giving it the appearance that it was unfinished, still in the process of being built. Yet the furniture was arranged in an orderly way, and there were carpets on the floor. Birds rustled in a cage near the kitchen door. On one of the walls there was a painting of the back of a woman in a tobe, balancing a basket on her head.

'One of yours?' Yassir asked, but Ronan said no, he did not like to hang his own paintings in the house.

'All my work is on the roof,' he said and from the kitchen he got a tray with a plastic jug full of kerkadeh and ice and three glasses. Some of the ice splashed into the glasses as he began to pour, and a pool of redness gathered in the tray, sliding slowly around in large patterns.

'You have a room on the roof?' Yassir asked.

'That's where I paint,' Ronan said. 'I lock it though, we've had many *haramiah* in the area. Not that they would steal my paintings but it's better to be careful. I'm in there most nights though, the *kahrabah* permitting.'

Hearing the Arabic words for 'thieves' and 'electricity'

made Yassir smile. He remembered Manaal copying the way Zahra's mother spoke. He wondered how well Ronan K. knew Arabic.

'My wife has the key. But she is right next door. The neighbours' daughter had a baby last week. There's a party of some kind there,' and he looked at Manaal as if for an explanation.

'A *simayah*,' she said.

'That's right,' said Ronan, 'a *simayah*. Maybe you could go over and get the key from her? It's right next door.'

'Is it Amna and her people?' Manaal asked him. 'I've seen them here before.'

'Yes, that's them.'

'Last time I was here, Amna walked in with chickens to put in your freezer. There wasn't enough room in theirs.'

'Chickens with their heads still on them and all the insides,' said Ronan. 'Terrible … This morning she brought over a leg of lamb,' and he gestured vaguely towards the kitchen.

'So who had the baby?' Manaal asked.

'Let's see if I can get this one right,' he said. 'The sister of Amna's husband, who happens to be – just to make things complicated – married to the cousin of Amna's mother.'

They laughed because Ronan gave an exaggerated sigh as if he had done a lot of hard work.

'I thought you said it was the neighbours' daughter,' said Yassir.

'Well this Amna character,' he said and Manaal laughed and nodded at the word 'character', 'she is living with her in-laws, so it is really the in-laws' house.'

Manaal got up to go and Ronan said, 'I'll tell you what. Just throw the keys up to us on the roof. We'll wait for you there. It will save time.'

The roof was dark and cool, its floor more uneven than the floor of the house had been. The ledge all around it was low, only knee-high. El-Ma'moura lay spread out before them, the half-built houses surrounded by scaffolding, piles of sand and discarded bricks. Shadows of stray dogs made their way through the rubble. Domes of cardboard marked the places where the caretakers of the houses and their families lived. Their job was to guard the bags of cement, the toilets, the tiles that came for the new houses. Once the houses were built they would linger, drawing water from the pipes that splashed on the embryonic streets, until they were eventually sent away.

From the house next door came the sounds of children playing football, scuffling, names called out loud. A woman's voice shrieked from indoors. Yassir and Ronan sat on the ledge. He offered Yassir a cigarette and Yassir accepted though he hadn't smoked for several years. Ronan put his box of matches between them. It had a picture of a crocodile on it, mouth wide open, tail arched up in the air. Yassir had forgotten how good it felt to strike a match, flick grey ash away. It was one of the things he and Emma had done together – given up smoking.

'A long way from Aberdeen, or rather Aberdeen is a long way from here,' Ronan said.

'Have you been there before?'

'I know it well, my mother originally came from Elgin. They can be a bit parochial up there, don't you think?'

At the back of Yassir's mind, questions formed and rose out of a sense of habit, but dropped languidly as if there was no fuel to vocalise them. What was this man doing here, in a place where even the nights were hot and alcohol was forbidden? Where there was little comfort and little material gain? The painter sat on his roof and, like the raised spots on the girl's face did not arouse his derision, Yassir felt only passive wonder.

'If you look this way,' Ronan said, 'you can see the airport – where the red and blue lights are. Sometimes I see the airplanes circling and landing. They pass right over me when they take off. I see the fat bellies of planes full of people going away. Last August we had so much rain. This whole area was flooded we couldn't drive to the main road. The Nile rose and I could see it with my telescope, even though it is far from here.'

'How long have you been here?' Yassir asked.

'Fifteen years.'

'That's a long time.'

Giant wisps of white brushed the sky as if the smoke from their cigarettes had risen high, expanded and stood still. Stars were pushing their way into view, gathering around them the darkest dregs of night. On the roof, speaking Emma's language for the first time in two weeks, Yassir missed her, not with the light eagerness he had known on the rigs but with something else, something plain and unwanted, the grim awareness of distance. He knew why he had wanted her to come with him, not to 'see', but so that Africa would move her, startle her, touch her in some irreversible way.

* * *

Manaal threw up the keys. Ronan opened the locked room and put the light on. It was a single bulb which dangled from the ceiling, speckled with the still bodies of black insects. The room smelled of paint, a large fan stood in the corner. Conscious of his ignorance, Yassir was silent as Ronan, cigarette drooping from his mouth, showed him one painting after the other. 'I like them,' he said, and it was true. They were clear and uncluttered, the colours light, giving an impression of sunlight. Most were of village scenes, mud houses, one of children playing with a goat, one of a tree that had fallen into the river.

'Paper is my biggest problem,' said Ronan. 'The brushes and paints last for quite some time. But if I know someone who is going abroad, I always ask them for paper.'

'Is it special paper that you need?'

'Yes, thicker for water colours.'

'I like the one of the donkey in front of the mud house,' said Yassir.

'The Hilton don't seem to want mud houses.'

'Did they tell you that?'

'No, I just got this feeling.'

'That means I could get them at a discount?'

'Maybe ... How many were you thinking of taking?'

Yassir choose three, one of them the children with the goat because he thought Samia might like that. He paid after some haggling. Downstairs the birds were asleep in their cage, there was no longer any ice in the jug of kerkadeh. Manaal was waiting for him by the gate. She had a handful of dates from next door which she offered to Ronan and Yassir. The dates were dry and cracked uncomfortably under Yassir's teeth before softening into sweetness. It was now time to leave. He shook hands with Ronan. The visit was a success – he had achieved what he came for.

* * *

Manaal slept in the car on the way home. Yassir drove through streets busier than the ones he had found in the afternoon. This was his last day in Khartoum. Tomorrow night a plane would take him to Paris, another plane to Glasgow, then the train to Aberdeen. Perhaps Ronan K. would be on his roof tomorrow night, watching Air France rise up over the new houses of El-Ma'moura.

The city was acknowledging his departure, recognising his need for a farewell. Headlamps of cars jerked in the badly lit streets, thin people in white floated like clouds. Voices, rumbling lorries, trucks leaning to one side snorting fumes. On a junction with a busier road, a small bus went past carrying a wedding party. It was lit inside, an orange light that caught the singing faces, the clapping hands. Ululations, the sound of a drum, lines from a song. Yassir drove on and gathered around him what he would take back with him, the things he could not deliver. Not the beads, not the paintings, but other things. Things devoid of the sense of their own worth. Manaal's silhouette against the rig's flare, against a sky dyed with kerkadeh. The scent of soap and shampoo in his car, a man picking his toenails, a page from a newspaper spread out as a mat. A voice that said, 'I see the planes circling at night, I see their lights, all the people going away. Manaal saying, 'You could have made it easier for her, you could have been more kind.'

The Ostrich

'You look like something from the Third World,' he said, and I let myself feel hurt, glancing downwards so that he would not see the look in my eyes. I didn't answer his taunting smile like he expected me to, didn't say, 'And where do you come from?' I let him put his arm around me by way of greeting and gave him the trolley with my suitcases to push.

He must have seen me first, I thought, while I was scanning the faces of the people who were waiting at the terminal, he must have been watching me all the time. And I suddenly felt ashamed, not only for myself, but for everyone else who arrived with me on that airplane. Our shabby luggage, our stammering in front of the immigration officer, our clothes that seemed natural a few hours back, now crumpled and out of place.

So I didn't tell him about the baby, though I imagined
I would tell him right away in the airport as soon as we
met. Nor did I confess that at times I longed not to return,
that in Khartoum I felt everything was real and our life in
London a hibernation.

I had to remember to walk next to him and not loiter
behind. I was reluctant to leave the other passengers. A
few hours ago we were a cohesive unit, smug and loud
at Khartoum airport, the lucky few heading north. In the
airplane we ate the same food, faced the same direction
and acknowledged each other with nods and small smiles.
Now we were to separate, dazzled by the bright lights of
the terminal, made humble by the plush carpeted floors,
chastened by the perfect announcements, one after the
other, words we could understand, meanings we could
not. From the vacuum of the terminal where all sound was
absorbed, we would disperse into the cloudy city and soon
forget the pride with which we bought our tickets and left
our home. He dislikes it if I walk a few steps behind him.
'What would people think,' he says, 'that we are backward,
barbaric.' He sneers at the Arab women in black abayas
walking behind their men. 'Oppressed, that's what people
would think of them. Here they respect women, treat them
as equal; we must be the same,' he says. So I have to be
careful not to fall behind him in step and must bear the
weight of his arm around my shoulder, another gesture he
had decided to imitate to prove that, though we are Arabs
and Africans, we can be modern too.

We waited outside the terminal for the Air Bus to arrive. Only two months away and I had forgotten how wet this country could be. Already my painted toes stuck out of my soaked sandals, a mockery. He looked well, he told me his research was progressing, he had been to Bath for a conference where his supervisor read a paper. 'It had an acknowledgement of me at the bottom of the first page,' he said, 'because I did the simulation work on the computer. In italics, the author thanks Majdy El-Shaykh and so on.'

Majdy will write his own papers one day, he will complete his PhD and have 'Dr' before his name. His early doubts, his fears of failure are receding. I should have felt proud. I supposed I would one day, but at that moment I felt tired and insincere. I strained to feel the baby move inside me, but there was only silence.

'You are envied, Samra,' my mother said, 'envied for living abroad where it is so much more comfortable than here. Don't complain, don't be ungrateful.' But when she saw the resentment on my face she softened and said, 'It will be easier when you have the baby. Something to fill your day, you won't have time to be homesick then.' Yet I imagined that I could just not come back, slip into my old life. Month after month and he would forget me in time, send me my divorce paper as an afterthought, marry someone else perhaps. He would marry an English woman with yellow hair and blue eyes. I catch him thinking that sometimes, if he had waited a little and not rushed into this marriage, he could have married a woman like the ones he admires on TV. We married so that he would not bring back a foreign wife like so many Sudanese students did, or worse, marry her and never come back. Who wants to go back to the Sudan after tasting the good life of the West? With a Sudanese wife though, he would surely come back. This is what his family told me, half in jest, half in earnest. So I was flattered with presents, a big wedding, a good-looking, educated bridegroom and the chance to go abroad. No reason for me to refuse. But perhaps they cannot twist fate; perhaps I am not strong enough to hold him to his roots.

* * *

'If I find a way to live here forever,' he says, 'if only I could get a work permit. I can't imagine I could go back, back to the petrol queue, to computers that don't have electricity to work on or paper to print on. Teach dim-witted students who never held a calculator in their hands before. And a salary, a monthly salary that is less than what an unemployed person gets here in a week! Calculate it if you don't believe me.'

He had answers to all the objections I raised. 'Morality, what morality do we have when our politicians are corrupt, when we buy arms to fuel a civil war instead of feeding the hungry? And don't talk of racism! We are more racist than the British – how have we Northerners always treated the Southern Sudanese?'

The bus came at last and we sat upstairs while the green countryside around Heathrow drifted past. The green leaves in Khartoum are a different green, sharper, drier, arrogant in the desert heat. I know this bus, I know this route; it is as familiar as a film one sees several times. Two years in London and when I come back after two months in Khartoum I feel like I am starting all over again. Two months wiped out two years, and I am a stranger once again.

'Did you meet anyone on the plane that you knew?' Majdy asked. One always does travelling to and from Khartoum, a small city with many familiar faces. I lied and said no. I lied and did not tell him that, on the first part of the journey from Khartoum to Cairo, I met the Ostrich.

I never could train myself to remember his real name. I always thought of him as the Ostrich and maybe I even called him that to his face, although I have no memory of his response. More likely I told my friends and was probably disappointed that they didn't start using that name too.

He really did look like an ostrich with his thin protruding neck and his long dangling arms. He walked head craned forward, eyebrows raised, taking wide, tentative steps. His hair was light in colour, sticking out in a large Afro that swayed when he moved, matted flat at the back of his head as if he was too lazy to reach that far with his comb. It was when we were in our second year at

university that he descended upon our class, after we had
sorted ourselves out into groups, after we had set labels
on each other. He should have been in his fourth year, but
he lost two years when a speeding car knocked him down.
His body healed, but his eyes were permanently damaged
and they remained large, bleary and unfocused. They
placed him in a world which he alone inhabited, where
everything was fuzzy and everyone saw him as unclearly
as he saw them.

'Your bags were so heavy,' Majdy was saying. 'Did you
have to pay excess?'

'No ... It's the grapefruit I got you and the white plaited
cheese that you like.'

'From the land of famine you bring me food.' Again
the mocking tone, but I knew he was pleased. They were
things he secretly missed.

'It's not as bad as they make it out to be here on TV, or
not in Khartoum anyway. Normal, I suppose, weddings,
funerals, but still a feeling of depression. Everything is so
expensive... and everyone wants to leave. Every family
I visited has someone abroad. In the Gulf, in Egypt, in
America. Remember your neighbours, Ali and Samir?'

'The ones with the white Mercedes.'

'Mercedes or not, they're away too. Ali in Bahrain
and Samir in Norway. Imagine Norway, and his sister
and her husband are busy filling in forms to immigrate to
Australia.' I laughed. It was like a scramble.

'That's what I keep telling you. There's no future back

there, and if people who were much better off than us aren't coping, how can we ever cope if we go back? I'm doing the right thing, sticking it out here in any way that I can.'

The Ostrich had a brother who worked in the Gulf. He sent him a watch that could beep. I remember the Ostrich bringing it up to his nose, twisting his face sideways so that he could peer at the time. It was a novelty for most of us, the first digital watch that we ever saw. The alarm would go off at the end of the lecture, a reminder to the teacher to end the class. We would giggle then, us girls sitting in the front row. We always had the front rows. We would reserve the seats in advance, throwing our exercise books on the desk, throwing extra books for our friends. There were hundreds of us in one class and we would sit on the painful wooden seats. Numb behinds, arms brushing arms, knees against knees. And I remember the girls who would come in late, their footsteps loud in the hushed room, walking up a few steps and slipping in beside their friends. The Ostrich always floated in late and sat at the back where the blackboard was out of focus and he could not take down any notes, where he poked pencils in his hair, his ears, his nose, and waited for his watch to beep. It never occurred to us to offer him a seat in front.

He never inspired the self-conscious concern reserved for the handicapped. We did not compete to offer him help and I remember him once telling me that I looked nice in blue, and I had laughed and asked him how he could tell or that he would say the same thing to a donkey, given the chance. I was cruel to him. Sometimes I looked into his eyes and they were beautiful, amber and mysterious like a newborn child's. Welcoming, like nests of whirling honey. Sometimes I felt sickened by their bleariness, the long eyelashes caked with sleep.

* * *

I had forgotten how small the flat was, how thin the walls were. Student accommodation. The cleanliness comes as a surprise, this clean land free of dust and insects. Everywhere carpet and everything compact; like boxes inside boxes, the houses stuck together defensively. September and it is already winter, already cold. The window, how many hours did I spend looking out of this window? For two years I looked out at strangers, unable to make stories about them, unable to tell who was rich and who was poor, who mended pipes and who healed the ill. And sometimes, disturbingly, not even knowing who was a man and who was a woman. Strangers I must respect, strangers who were better than me. This is what Majdy says. Every one of them is better than us. See the man who is collecting the rubbish; he is not ravaged by malaria, anaemia, bilharzia; he can read the newspaper, write a letter; he has a television in his house and his children go to a school where they get taught from glossy books. And if they are clever, if they show a talent in music or science, they will be encouraged and they might be important people one day. I look at the man who collects the rubbish and I am ashamed that he picks bags with our filth in them. When I pass him on the road, I avert my eyes.

And now that I am back, the room rises up to strangle me. The window beckons and it is already dark outside. I was wrong to return. All the laughter and confidence has been left behind. What am I doing here? A stranger suddenly appearing on the stage with no part to play, no lines to read. Majdy points out the graffiti for me, 'Black Bastards' on the wall of the mosque, 'Paki go home' on the newsagent's door. 'Do you know what it means, who wrote it?' I breed a new fear of not knowing, never knowing who these enemies are. How would I recognise them while they can so easily recognise me? The woman who sells me stamps (she is old, I must respect her age), the librarian who could not spell my name while the queue behind me grew (I will be reading her books for free), or the bus driver I angered by not giving him the correct change (it's my fault, I must obey the sign on the door). Which one of them agrees with what's written on the walls?

There are others, Majdy's new friends. 'So-and-so is good,' he says, 'friendly.' He invites them here, men with kind eyes and women who like the food I cook. But I must be wary, there are things I mustn't say when they are here. I mentioned polygamy once saying we shouldn't condemn something that Allah had permitted, remarking that Majdy's father had a second wife. When they left he slapped me, and, fool that I was, I didn't understand what I had done wrong.

'Why, why,' I asked and he slapped me more.

'It's worse when you don't understand,' he said. 'At least have a feeling that you have said something wrong. They can forgive you for your ugly colour, your thick lips and rough hair, but you must think modern thoughts, be like them on the inside if you can't be from the outside.' And what stuck in my mind after the stinging ebbed away, after the apologetic caresses, what clung to me and burned me time and time again were his comments about how I looked. I would stand in front of the mirror and, Allah forgive me, hate my face.

'You look beautiful in blue,' the Ostrich said, and when I was cruel he said, 'but I can be a judge of voices can I not?' I didn't ask him what he thought of my voice. I walked away. It must have been in the evening that I was wearing blue. It was white tobes in the morning, coloured ones for the evening. The evening lectures were special, leisurely; there was time after lunch to shower, to have a nap. To walk from the hostels in groups and pairs, past the young boy selling peanuts, past the closed post office, past the neem trees with the broken benches underneath. Jangly earrings, teeth smacking chewing gum and kohl in our eyes. The tobes slipping off our carefully combed hair, lifting our hands, putting them back on again. Tightening the material, holding it under our left arm. I miss these gestures, already left behind. Majdy says, 'If you cover your hair in London they'll think I am forcing you to do that. They won't believe it is what you want.' So I must walk unclothed, imagining cotton on my hair, lifting my hand to adjust an imaginary tobe.

The sunset prayers were a break in the middle of these evening lectures. One communist lecturer, keen to assert his atheism, ignored the rustling of the notebooks, the shuffling of restless feet, the screech of the Ostrich's alarm. Only when someone called out, 'A break for the prayers!' did he stop teaching. I will always see the grass, patches of dry yellow, the rugs of palm fibre laid out. They curl at the edges and when I put my forehead on the ground I can smell the grass underneath. Now that we have a break we must hurry, for it is as if the birds have heard the *azan* and started to pray before us. I can hear their praises, see the branches bow down low to receive them as they dart to the trees. We wash from a corner tap, taking turns. The Ostrich squats and puts his whole head under the tap. He shakes it backwards and drops of water balance on top of his hair. I borrow a mug from the canteen and I am proud, a little vain knowing that I can wash my hands, face, arms and feet with only one mug. Sandals discarded, we line up and the boy from the canteen joins us, his torn clothes stained with tea. Another lecturer, not finding room on the mat, spreads his handkerchief on the grass. If I was not praying I would stand with my feet crunching the gravel stones and watch the straight lines, the men in front, the colourful tobes behind. I would know that I was part of this harmony, that I needed no permission to belong. Here in London, the birds pray discreetly and I pray alone. A printed booklet, not a muezzin, tells me the times. Here in London, Majdy does not pray. 'This country,' he says, 'chips away at your faith bit by bit.'

* * *

There were unwashed dishes in the sink, fragile eggshells to throw away, dirty socks on the floor. On Majdy's desk – empty mugs of tea, the twisted cores of apples. I started to tidy up; he switched on the TV. Computer printouts lay on piles on the floor. Many evenings before I went to Khartoum, he would work at his desk while I sat and cut the perforated edges of the sheets, strings of paper with holes. I played with them in my hands, twisting them into shapes, making bracelets and rings like a child. And these were the happy moments of our marriage, when the world outside was forgotten, when his concentration in his work was so intense that he would whistle the tunes of Sudanese songs we knew long ago.

Two months have yielded plenty of computer printouts. When I tidied up, when I unpacked, when he switched off the television and settled at his desk with a mug of tea, a feast awaited me. A feast of the sounds of paper separating from paper, holes settling upon holes, chains of entwined crispness. Now I could sit on the floor with the paper in front of me, lean my back on Majdy's chair and unroll my memories. The Ostrich sitting on the bumper of a car parked inside the university, a number of us around him, standing against its windows. Notebooks in our arms, those thin notebooks with a spiral wire holding the pages, a drawing of the university on the front cover. What was the weather like? Hot, very hot – we can smell each other's sweat. Or one of those bright winter days when the sun softens its blows and a breeze whispers around the trees. Dust on the car, inside it; dust clinging to the Ostrich's hair, dust climbing between our toes. The shadows of the tree dance around the Ostrich, elusive patches of shade. What did we speak of in those days, when everything seemed possible and we were naive, believing the university an end not a means? 'Some emir in the Gulf bought a horse in England for ten million pounds. Imagine ten million in hard currency. It could have built a hospital, schools, roads. Shoes for me,' says the Ostrich stretching his feet, his sandals torn, his toes coarse and gnarled, feet that could withstand burning tiles ... 'Wish for a coup, the first thing they'll do is close the university, or better still a reason for a strike a month or so before the exams. Postponement and no Fiscal Policy... What has that man been going on about all year? Swear I saw last year's paper and couldn't even tell which parts of the lecture notes the answers came from.'

Cinnamon tea, sweet in chipped glasses. Roasted watermelon seeds, the salt dissolving in our mouths, the empty shells falling around like leaves. The Ostrich, a forgotten shell on his lip, slides down from the car's bumper, raises his arms, head back and turns around in circles. Under his arms there are patches of wetness. His weak eyes brave the midday sun. Laughter bubbles inside him letting loose the shell from his lip. 'The fan,' he says, laughing more, bending forward and slapping his hands together. 'The fan in the common room fell down from the ceiling. You should have seen it. It went whizzing around the room like a spinning top.' We exclaim, we ask questions, no one was hurt, hardly anyone was in the room at the time. He found it funny. Perhaps this is the essence of my country, what I miss most. Those everyday miracles, the poise between normality and chaos. The awe and the breathtaking gratitude for simple things. A place where people say, 'Allah alone is eternal.'

* * *

I weave paper ribbons with holes, chains; the edges of each sheet are sharp. Grapefruit juice – no one buys for themselves alone, always sharing, competing in generosity (our downfall, Majdy says, the downfall of a whole people, a primitive tribal mentality and so inefficient). Pink grapefruit juice, frothy at the top, jagged pieces of ice struck out of large slabs with particles of sand frozen inside. 'Am Ali, the man who makes the juice has to hold down the cover of the mixer. He can make only two glasses at a time and when the electricity fails he can make none.

Aubergine sandwiches, the baked plant crushed to a pulp, red hot with pepper, the bread in thin loaves. Bread is rationed now. I stood in a queue for bread every morning in the two months I was back in Khartoum.

Coming across the Ostrich in the library, his nose literally in a large book. Not on Cost-Benefit Analysis, Rostow's take-off, Pareto's curves, not for him. He would be reading poetry from old, musty books that perhaps no one looked at except him. He once looked up at me as I passed, his eyes bulging from the strain he was putting them through. He quoted the Andalusian poet Ibn Zaydun, 'Yes, I have remembered you with longing, at al-Zahra, when the horizon was bright and the face of the earth gave pleasure, and the breeze was soft in the late afternoon, as if it had pity on me.' I smiled at him then, wondering if he could see my smile, knowing he was memorising the poem.

* * *

The Ostrich picked his nose on prime time television. What he dislodged, he rolled leisurely between his thumb and forefinger like a grain of rice. Held it up, peered at it closely, narrowing his eyes before flicking it away. We hooted with laughter as we crowded around the black and white TV set of the girls' hostel, cross-legged on the floor, on each other's laps on wobbling metal chairs, Vaseline glistening on our arms and rollers in our hair. It was a game show, a poetry competition with the flamboyant title, *Knights in the Arena*. When a competitor recites a verse, his opponent must recite one that starts with the last letter of the last word in that verse. The skill was in memory and the ability to throw verses at your opponent, which end with the same letter, depleting his particular stock.

The Ostrich excelled. Leaning back on his chair, his fingers in his nose and in his ears, oblivious to the cameras, to the hundreds who were watching, he gave us the poetry of the pre-Islamic Arabs, their pride in the strength of their tribe. Lovers weeping at the remains of the camp fires from which their beloved had gone away, the Sufi poems of self-annihilation and longing to join the Almighty.

Alienated in his own hazy world, the Ostrich was free. And when he won the prize of fifty pounds and a trophy, he took as many of us as he could to a restaurant by the Nile, where we ate kebabs and watched the moon's reflection flutter in the running water below.

⁎ ⁎ ⁎

It was late. Footsteps no longer sounded in the corridor outside, the heating had gone off and it was cold. I went to get my shawl from the bedroom; it was folded in the cupboard just as I had left it weeks ago. I wrapped it around me and sat cross-legged again on the floor. In the final exams the Ostrich sat next to me in the hall. 'Number three,' he whispered, 'number three,' his head on top of his paper, his eyes strangely oscillating. I saw the invigilator look up towards him, towards us. I had helped him before, lending him my notes, nagging him for days to bring them back only to discover he had passed them on to someone else, and in the exams where we always seemed to sit next to each other, whispering a few helpful words here and there whenever I got the chance. That last time though, I peeled my hand off my paper and saw that the ink had been smudged, the paper made thin by my sweat. (Typical inefficiency, Majdy would say, he should have been specially examined, someone reading out the questions to him, noting down his answers). 'Shut up,' I whispered back, 'shut up,' and when the invigilator walked past, I stopped him and complained about the Ostrich. They moved him away, he protested, his eyes darting wildly as if he could not hold them still. He swore; they were harsh and dragged him away. His chair remained overturned next to me until the end of the exam. 'Why,' my friends asked me, 'why tell on him like that?' I graduated, he did not, and for years I did not see him until I met him today on the airplane.

But it was not today anymore, it was yesterday for the watch on my wrist showed 2am – midnight London time. I moved the hands slowly, pushing time back. Majdy looked tired from too much concentration. There were shiny dark grooves under his eyes. He picked the pile of printouts from the floor, bald of their edges, and began to tidy them up, sort them out into piles. Some he will not want at all; I will use them to line up drawers and give them to the daughter of the Malaysian couple who live on the ground floor. She likes to draw on them.

'I was afraid you wouldn't come back,' Majdy suddenly said. And I wondered if this was the right time, so late at night, to talk of such things, things that would drive the sleep from our eyes. When I looked at him, he seemed weak and this made him look more beautiful than he had looked at the airport. I remembered the stories his sisters told me about how he was when he first came here. Despairing of ever passing his exams, of ever catching up with the work. And now he was nearly through. The rescue package his family sent him has achieved its purpose. 'I work better when you are next to me,' he was saying. 'It is easier to keep awake. When I saw you in the airport today, you brought back many memories to me. Of people I love and left behind, of what I once was years ago. I envy you and you find that funny, don't you, but it's true. I envy you because you are displaced yet intact, unchanged, while I question everything and I am not sure of anything anymore.'

And it was only then, late that night, when he came and sat near me on the floor that I told him about our baby.

* * *

That night I dreamt of the Ostrich's bride. She was, like she had told me on the airplane, at university with me. In the dream, we were in one of the lecture rooms, the fans circling above our head. I made a chain from the perforated edges of the computer paper and gave it to her. She wore it as an ankle bracelet and I was anxious that the paper might tear, but she laughed at my fears.

It was the Ostrich who recognised me first on the airplane. 'Samra,' he said, and when I looked blankly at him, trying to find the way to my seat, 'Don't you remember me, Samra?' His hair was cut short, his eyes behind dark spectacles and I could tell that he was newly married. From the henna intricately designed on his bride's palms, from the gold bracelets on her arms, the shimmering material of her new tobe, I could tell they were on their honeymoon. We exchanged news the way people do when they have not met for a long time. Is this happiness then, the sudden rush of recognition, the warmth, the shy laughter? Swapping news of others that we mutually knew. Could I have ever believed that the word happiness can be cramped in a few minutes, a few unexpected minutes in the aisle of an airplane?

'My brother set up a video shop in Medani, which I run,' the Ostrich said and we both laughed again, as if it was something funny, as if we shared a private joke. 'Hindi films are popular,' he rambled in his Ostrich way. 'Nobody understands the language but they keep renting out the films.'

'I remember you from university,' she interrupted us. 'I was in my first year when you were in your last.' Her confident smile, her almost flirty manner. I disliked her for making him hide his eyes and cut his hair. And it was uncomfortable trying to remember her face, vaguely familiar though it was, trying to suppress a hurt vanity at the reminder of the disparity in our ages.

Envy is more unwelcome than grief. It took me unaware, tripped me and I fell into a pool of thoughts that were unreasonable, that should never have been mine. Would she sit on his lap and clean his eyelashes with her manicured hands? Would he write her notes in his large handwriting, the grotesque letters uncontrolled by the lines he couldn't see?

In my seat with the hum of the aircraft in my ears, I fought my morning sickness and watched the clouds out of the window swirl around. She passed me twice, leaving behind a faint smell of sandalwood, a tinkle of her bracelets, a raised eyebrow, an attractive smile. She looked familiar because she was like a younger version of myself. When the airplane landed in Cairo, they said goodbye. No addresses exchanged, no promises made. New passengers boarded and took their place, an Egyptian lady and her daughter who kept writing in a small notebook. And when the airplane took off again, I left the Ostrich and Africa behind me as I had done once before.

Majed

'What are you doing?' Hamid couldn't see her properly because he didn't have his glasses on. She was blurred over the kitchen sink, holding the bottle in her hand. She was not supposed to be holding that bottle. How did she get hold of it? He had hidden it behind the DVDs late last night. He had washed his glass carefully over the kitchen sink, gargled with ASDA Protect then crept into bed beside her, careful, very careful not to wake her or the two youngest ones. Majed slept in the cot in the corner of the room, the newborn baby slept with them in the double bed so that Ruqiyyah could feed her during the night. During the night when Hamid had to go to the toilet he tried to be careful not to wake them up. Though sometimes he did, bumping into Majed's cot, stumbling on a toy. One night he had found himself, almost too late, not in the toilet but surrounded by the shoes that littered the entrance to the flat. He was startled into full consciousness by the baby crying.

'Ruqiyyah, what are you doing?' He should make a lunge at her, stop her before it was too late. It was precious stuff she was threatening to pour down the drain. But the whole household was in his way. A pile of washing waiting to go into the washing machine, the baby, sunk down and small, in her seat on the floor. She was creamy and delicate, wearing tiny gloves so that she would not scratch herself. The kitchen table was in his way. Majed sat on his high chair covered in porridge, singing, banging the table with his spoon, Sarah talked to him and chewed toast. Robin scooped Rice Krispies into his mouth while staring at the box; Snap, Crackle and Pop flying and things you could send for if your parents gave you the money.

Ruqiyyah put the bottle down. But only because there were plates and baby bottles in the sink. She started to wash them up, water splashing everywhere.

She looked at Hamid and shook her head.

Hamid groaned. He was relieved he couldn't see her eyes, her blue eyes filled with tears maybe. She had not always been Ruqiyyah, she once was someone else with an ordinary name, a name a girl behind the counter in the Bank of Scotland might have. When she became Muslim she changed her name then left her husband. Robin and Sarah were not Hamid's children. Ruqiyyah had told Hamid horror stories about her previous marriage. She had left little out. When she went on about her ex-husband, Hamid felt shattered. He had never met Gavin (who wanted nothing to do with Ruqiyyah, Robin and Sarah and had never so much as sent them a bean), but that man stalked Hamid's nightmares. Among Hamid's many fears, was the fear of Gavin storming the flat, shaking him until his glasses fell off, 'You filthy nigger, stay away from my family.'

'Ruqiyyah, wait, I'll get my glasses.' He looked at the children. He looked back at her, made a face. When the children finished their breakfast and headed towards Children's TV, they could talk. They couldn't talk in front of Robin. He was old enough to understand, pick up things. He was sensitive. Hamid ruffled Robin's hair, said something jolly about Snap, Crackle and Pop. Robin smiled and this encouraged Hamid to be more jocular. Whenever Hamid was stressed, he changed into a clown. The hahaha of laughter covered problems. Hahaha had wheels, it was a skateboard to slide and escape on.

'I'll get my glasses.' He stumbled away. He needed the glasses. The glasses would give him confidence. He would be able to talk, explain. She was so good, so strong, because she was a convert. But he, he had been a Muslim all his life and was, it had to be said, relaxed about the whole thing. Wrong, yes it was wrong. He wasn't going to argue about that. Not with Ruqiyyah. Instead he would say ... he would explain, that on the scale ... yes on the scale (he was a scientist after all and understood scales), on the scale of all the forbidden things, it was not really so wrong, so bad. There were worse, much worse, the heavies, the Big Ones: black magic, adultery, abusing your parents (something the dreadful Gavin had done – *pushed the old dear round her living room* – may he rot in Hell on account of this for all eternity and more). Hamid would explain ... Once he put his glasses on and the world cleared up he would explain. Human weakness etc., and Allah is all forgiving. That's right. Then a sad, comic face. A gentle hahaha. But she could counter that argument about forgiveness though. He must be careful. She would say that one has to repent first before one could be forgiven. And she would be right. Of course. Absolutely. He had every intention to repent. *Every* intention. But not now, not this minute, not today. A few more days, when he got himself sorted out, when this bottle was finished, when he finished his PhD, when he got a proper job and did not need to work evenings in ASDA.

He found his glasses near the bed between the baby lotion and the zinc and castor oil. He put them on and felt better, more focused, more in control. Ruqiyyah hadn't yet dealt with this room. There were nappies on the floor, folded up and heavy. She had, though, stripped the sheets off Majed's cot. There were soft cartoon characters on the plastic mattress. Hamid rescued the prayer mat off the nappy-covered floor and dropped it on the unmade bed. He opened the window for the smells in the room to go out and fresh air to come in.

Outside was another grey day, brown leaves all over the

pavements. A gush of rainy air, a moment of contemplation. *Subhan Allah*, who would have ever thought that he, Hamid, born and bred on the banks of the Blue Nile, would end up here with a Scottish wife, who was a better Muslim than he was. Why had he married her? Because of the residence visa, to solve his problem with the Home Office once and for all. A friend had approached him once after Friday prayers (he did sometimes go to the mosque for Friday prayers, he was not *so* useless), and told him about Ruqiyyah, how she was a new convert with two little ones, how she needed a husband to take care of her. And you Hamid, need a visa ... Why not? Why not? Ha ha. Is she pretty? Ha ha. There had been a time in Hamid's life when the only white people he saw were on the cinema screen, now they would be under one roof. Why not? He brushed his teeth with enthusiasm, sprayed himself with Old Spice, armed himself with the jolly laugh and set out to meet the three of them.

Robin's shy face, the gaze of a child once bitten twice shy. A woman of average height, with bright anxious blue eyes, her hair covered with a black scarf, very conservatively dressed, no make-up. He breathed a sigh of relief that she was not lean like European women tended to be. Instead she was soft like his own faraway mother, like a girl he had once longed for in the University of Khartoum, a girl who had been unattainable. And if on that first meeting, Ruqiyyah's charms were deliberately hidden, they were obvious in her one-year-old daughter.

Sarah was all smiles and wavy yellow hair, stretching out her arms, wanting to be carried, wanting to be noticed. After the awkwardness of their first meeting, a lot of hahaha, tantrums from Robin, desperate jokes, Hamid stopped laughing. He entered that steady place under laughter. He fell in love with the three of them, their pale needy faces, the fires that were repressed in them. His need for a visa, her need for security, no longer seemed grasping or callous. They were swept along by the children, his own children coming along, tumbling out soon, easily. Two years ago Majed, three weeks ago the baby. At school when Ruqiyyah and Majed went to pick up Robin, no one believed that they were brothers. Ruqiyyah with her children: two Europeans, two Africans. The other mothers outside the school looked at her oddly, smiled too politely. But Ruqiyyah could handle the other mothers, she had been through much worse. She had once escaped Gavin to a Women's Refuge, lived with rats and Robin having a child's equivalent of a nervous breakdown.

He must make it to the kitchen before she poured the Johnny Walker down the sink. He was angry. His secret was out and now that it was out it could not go back in again. It wasn't fair. If she was suspicious why hadn't she turned a blind eye, why had she searched for the proof? It wasn't fair. These were his private moments, late at night, all by himself, the children asleep, Ruqiyyah asleep. The whole soft sofa to himself, a glass of whisky in his hand, the television purring sights that held his attention, kung fu, football, Sumo wrestling, Prince Naseem thrashing someone. Anything that blocked out the thesis, the humiliating hours spent mopping up ASDA's floor, the demanding, roving kids. Anything cheerful, not the news, definitely not the news. The last thing he wanted at that time of night were his brothers and sisters suffering in the West Bank. His own warm, private moments, the little man on the bottle of Johnny Walker. That little man was Johnny, an average sort of guy and because he was walking, striding along with his top hat, he was a Walker, Johnny Walker. Or perhaps because he *was* Johnny Walker, he was represented as walking, striding along happily. It was interesting, but at the end it didn't matter and that was what Hamid wanted at that time of night. Things that didn't matter. At times he took his glasses off, let the television become a blur, and he would become a blur too, a hazy, warm, lovable blur. Nothing sharp, nothing definite. The exact number of years he had been a PhD student. Don't count, man, don't count. Laughter blurred things too. Hahaha. His thesis was not going to make it. He must, his supervisor said, stretch himself. His thesis now, as it stood, was *not meaty enough*. There was a lot of meat in ASDA, shelves of it. When he cleaned underneath them, he shivered from the cold. Not meaty enough. Johnny Walker was slight and not at all meaty and he was alright, successful, striding along brimming with confidence. Why shouldn't a man with an unfinished thesis and an ego-bashing job at ASDA sit up late at night, once in a while, settle down in front of the television and sink in. Sink into the warmth of the whisky and the froth of the TV. Once in a while?

Majed lunged into the room. He squealed when he saw Hamid sitting on the bed. 'Majed, say *salaam*, shake hands.' Hamid held his hand out. Majed took his fist out of his mouth and placed it, covered in saliva, in his father's hand. Then he pointed to his cot, transformed because the sheet wasn't on it. It wasn't often that Ruqiyyah changed the sheets. Majed walked over to his cot mumbling exclamations of surprise. He put his hands through the bars and patted the cartoon characters on the plastic mattress. 'Mummy's washing your sheet. You'll be getting a nice clean sheet,' Hamid said. It was rare that the two of them were alone together. Hamid held him up and hugged him, put him on his lap. He loved him so much. He loved his smell and roundness, his tight little curls and wide forehead. Majed was a piece of him, a purer piece of him. And that love was a secret because it was not the same love he felt for Robin and Sarah. He feared for Majed, throat-catching fear, while with Sarah and Robin he was calm and sensible. He dreamt about Majed. Majed crushed under a bus and Hamid roaring from the pain, which came from deep inside, which surfaced into sobs, then Ruqiyyah's voice, her hand on his cheeks, what's wrong, what's the matter and the wave of shame with the silent coolness of waking up. I'm sorry, I'm sorry, it's nothing, go back to sleep. The more he loved Majed and the newborn baby, the kinder Hamid was to Robin and Sarah. He must not be unjust. Ruqiyyah must never feel that he favoured their children over Robin and Sarah. It was a rare, precious moment when he was alone with Majed, no one watching them. He threw him up in the air and Majed squealed and laughed. He stood Majed on the bed and let him run, jump, fly from the bed into his outstretched arms. Then he remembered Ruqiyyah in the kitchen. The memory dampened the fun. He sent Majed off to join Sarah and Robin in front of the television and he walked back to the kitchen.

Ruqiyyah was clearing the things off the kitchen table, the baby was asleep in her chair on the floor. With his glasses on now, Hamid could clearly see the whisky bottle. Two thirds empty, two thirds ... His heart sank, that much ... or had she already poured some out? No. No, she hadn't. He knew what she was going to do. She was going to clear the kitchen, wash everything and put it away, then ceremoniously tip the bottle into the empty sink.

She started cleaning up Majed's high-chair. Her hair fell over her eyes. She wore an apron with Bugs Bunny on it. She was beautiful, not like women on TV, but with looks that would have been appreciated in another part of the world, in another century. Her lips were naturally red. He had thought, before they got married, that she was wearing lipstick. She wore hijab when she went out, she got up at dawn and prayed. This seriousness that he didn't have, baffled him. Something Scottish she brought with her when she stepped into Islam. The story of her conversion amazed him as much as her stories about Gavin shocked and sickened him. She had read books about Islam. Books Gavin had snatched and torn up. Not because they were about Islam, but because she was sitting on her fat arse reading instead of doing what he wanted her to do.

She wanted to learn Arabic. Hamid would doze in bed and next to him she would hold *Simple Words in Arabic*, over the head of the baby she was feeding. 'How do you say this?' she would ask from time to time, nudging him awake. When Hamid read Qur'an out loud (he went through religious spells in Ramadan and whenever one of the children fell ill), she said, 'I wish I could read like you.'

He started to help her tidy up. He closed the flaps on the box of Rice Krispies, put it away in the cupboard. When she finished wiping the table and started on the floor, he lifted up the baby's seat and put it on the table. If she would talk to him, shout at him it would be better. Instead he was getting this silent treatment. He began to feel impatient. What had made her search for the bottle? A smell ...?

Attack is the best form of defence. Laughter blurs things, smoothes them over. Hahaha. He began to talk, he put on his most endearing voice, tried a joke. Hahaha. She didn't answer him, didn't smile. She pushed her hair away from her face, poured powder into the drawer of the washing machine. She bent down and began to load the washing into the machine. It was linen, the sheets that had been on Majed's cot. Hamid said, 'But how did you know? Tell me.'

She sat on her heels, closed the door of the washing machine. She said, 'You pissed in Majed's cot. You thought you were in the toilet.' She twisted the dial that started the wash cycle, 'I pretended to be asleep. He didn't wake up.'

There is a place under laughter, under the hahaha.

Hamid saw her stand up, pick up the Johnny Walker and pour what was left of it down the drain. She poured it carefully so that not a single drop splashed on the sink where later the children's bowls and bottles would wait to be washed.

The Boy from the Kebab Shop

The sign was on the door of the computer room.

MUSLIM STUDENTS' SOCIETY
FUND RAISING FOR SYRIA TALK & DINNER
TIME: TONIGHT 6:00PM VENUE: CHAPLAINCY CENTRE

Dina went for the food. She arrived late and walked in as
some people were leaving. Those who hadn't yet left were
finishing their dinner, eating curry and rice off paper plates
with plastic spoons. Not everyone was sitting around a
table; some were sitting on chairs with plates on their laps,
some were sitting on the floor. A few children ran around,
climbed on the chairs and jumped off. The majority of
people in the room were young students, though there
were some mature students and a few middle-aged. Many

of the girls were wearing headscarves, some were wearing shalwar kameez – others like Dina wore the student outfit of jeans, sweatshirt and outrageous shoes. She joined the queue for the dinner. It was not a long queue.

Kassim scooped the lumpy, unpopular rice from a crate (which was actually a plastic box for storing toys), put it on a paper plate and said again, 'We've run out of chapattis.' With a soup ladle, he dished out curry from a huge pot. The last spoonfuls were thick with bits of chicken and pulverised potatoes. For the third time that evening, a student cut the queue and dumped his uneaten food in front of Kassim.

'I can't eat this rice.' The student wore an Adidas sweatshirt and glasses, 'It's not cooked. Look at it, stuck in lumps …'

'I'm sorry …' Kassim scooped the last piece of cucumber from the salad bowl and gave the plate to the young boy who was standing in front of Dina in the queue. The boy gave him a five-pound note and Kassim stuffed it in a Flora margarine container that was full of coins and notes. The boy didn't want any change.

'Give me chapattis instead of the rice,' said the student.

'We've run out of chapattis.'

'You've run out of chapattis, you're running out of chicken, what sort of organising is this? Every single function we have, there's something or other wrong with the food. You people can never get it right.' He walked away, hungry and angry.

Kassim put rice on Dina's plate. He stirred the ladle in the pot of curry searching for a piece of chicken. He said, 'It's mostly gravy now.'

'Doesn't matter.' She noticed that he looked scruffy and clean at the same. Scruffy because of his beard and longish hair.

'I've found a wing,' he looked up at her. 'I'm sorry there's no salad left.'

She shrugged and put two pounds fifty into the Flora box.

* * *

Now that there was no one else to serve, Kassim wiped the table, put away the unused paper plates and the bag of plastic spoons. He shook open a black rubbish bag and started to move around the room, picking up empty paper plates and cups. Basheer was stacking up the chairs. Heavily built and with greying hair, it always surprised Kassim how quickly and efficiently he worked.

'Did the complaint reach you?' Kassim asked. Basheer nodded and continued with his work. 'Well?'

'There has to be complaints. *Alhamdulillah* the auction raised a thousand pounds. And they still haven't counted the donations yet. It's been a success.'

Basheer's wife, Samia, interrupted them. She carried a large plastic bowl. Her one-year-old son clung at her skirt, whining. 'We'll put all the leftovers here and then give it to the birds. We can't throw all this away.' She put the bowl on one of the tables.

True enough, the chicken bones were clean but most of the plates had remains of rice. Kassim began pushing the uneaten rice into the bowl before dumping the paper plate into the bag. As he moved away he heard Samia say to Basheer, 'Leave these chairs for Kassim; you'll just make your back worse.'

* * *

Kassim reached the table next to where Dina was sitting. 'Did you like the talk early on?' he asked her.

'I missed it.'

He nodded. 'Me too, I was cooking the rice.'

'It's good,' she said, swallowing another mouthful. She was not discerning. Her mother, Shushu, rarely cooked proper meals because she was always on a diet. Shushu imposed these diets on her daughter too who was even more overweight. The dieting made Dina continuously peckish, uneasy. She often binged on crisps and Mars bars, and the diets inevitably failed but they were never officially abandoned. Dieting had become a way of life, part of the house, part of the mother-daughter relationship. Whenever Dina found an opportunity like tonight, away from her mother, she devoured the food, indiscriminately.

'I work in a kebab shop,' Kassim said. He nodded towards Basheer, 'He owns the shop. The meal tonight is a donation.'

Kassim pushed more paper plates in the bag and tied it up. He hauled the bag away.

By the time Dina finished her plate, the only people left in the room were Kassim, Basheer, another man, Samia and her toddler. Most of the chairs were stacked and put away. Kassim was wiping the tables with a cloth and the other man had started to hoover. The machine was old and the hose kept breaking off.

Because they were the only two women in the room, Samia came over and sat with Dina. With her son whining and the sound of the vacuum cleaner, conversation was difficult. Samia picked up her baby and shifted her chair so that her back was to the men in the room.

'Tell me if anyone comes,' she said and Dina couldn't quite understand what she meant.

She did a minute later when Samia lifted up her jumper, pulled down her bra and started to breastfeed her baby. He became instantly quiet – this was what he had been whining for.

As an average British girl of eighteen, Dina had seen plenty of nudity but she had never seen a woman breastfeed a baby. Now she was taken aback, slightly repulsed. Samia was a large woman; her loose clothes gave her a tomboyish look. The white scarf that covered her hair made her eyes dark and luminous. She smelt faintly of sweat and cooking spices. Feeding her baby, she definitely did not look like an antiseptic mum in a television ad for Pampers. The baby, Dina thought, was too old for this. She could hear him breathing from the effort of sucking, could hear him swallow, draw in the flow of milk, swallow. She looked away, not wanting this intimacy, shrinking away from what was fleshy and vulnerable. In this modern age, Dina was not psyched up for birth or motherhood. C++ was on her mind, and whether she should or should not, like her best friend Alanna, pierce her tongue or tattoo a butterfly on her arm.

Samia suddenly became chatty and inquisitive. Questions that Dina answered dully because she was mesmerised by the child, who was now dozing in his mother's arms, sucking himself to sleep, well fed.

This was the information that Samia got out of Dina. Dina was an IT student. Her mother was Egyptian, her father Scottish. Her father had died recently, from lung cancer. Her mother worked as a beautician in a department store. Dina's ties to Islam were fragile and distant. No, she had never been to Egypt. Shushu's family had disowned her when she married a Scot.

'Half Scottish, half Arab,' murmured Samia. 'That's like Kassim, but he's the other way round. His mother is Scottish and his father Moroccan.' Her baby let go of her nipple and suddenly snored loudly, his mouth wide open. Samia laughed and hitched up her bra, kissed her baby's forehead and pulled down her jumper. Dina laughed too – it made her feel less embarrassed.

* * *

Dina walked into the sitting room, which was dark except for the light of the television screen. Shushu was slumped on the sofa as if asleep. There was a bottle of gin on the coffee table, a glass, a packet of Panadol. Dina bent down over her mother, knelt down and touched her hair.

'Mum.'

Shushu's response was garbled. She turned her head away. There was mascara running down her face. Her breath, when she started to cry, was dry and sour.

'Mum, what happened? Did anything happen at work?' Shushu shook her head.

Dina sat on the floor and waited. She watched the black and white Egyptian film that was on Nile TV. It would have been romantic, or at least sad if Shushu was mourning her husband. But she had despised him and despised him until he had shrivelled into his grave. The good-looking *khawagah*, who had pursued and enchanted her in the Gezira Club, had whisked her off her feet and away from her family, had brought her to a drab life, in a drab place. In Scotland, he lost the charisma that Africa bestows on the white man, and became the average, kind-hearted father that Dina grew up with. A man who liked to go the pub, watch the football, dream of winning the lottery and not much else. Shushu expressed it now. She raised her arm up in the air, unsteadily, but brought it down hard to thud on the carpet.

'Whoosh.' It was all in that word, in the slender arm falling down onto the carpet. 'Everything shrunk when your father brought me here.'

'Go to bed,' said Dina. She had heard all this before; none of it was new. 'Don't get yourself all upset.'

'My sister won't send me the money.'

'That's why you're upset?'

'I spoke to her on the phone,' Shushu sat up on the couch. Her hair was dishevelled. 'My sister has a flat in Mohandisin. She has two maids doing all the work. Imagine two maids. And yet she grudges me, what is actually mine, my inheritance from my mother.'

'Hmm.'

'It was a black day when I first saw your father.'

They watched the film until the end. Nile TV was good for Dina because it had English subtitles on most of the films and so she could follow them. Sometimes, but not often, Shushu would make comments about the actors or the plot, give Dina snippets of information about Egyptian culture. Comments that were acerbic and surprisingly witty. Dina treasured them.

'Mum,' said Dina hesitantly, when the words *Al Nihaya* filled the screen, accompanied by a flourish of music. 'I phoned AA. They said I could come with you to a meeting, if you were too shy to go on your own.' Shushu waved her hand dismissively. She lay down again on the couch.

'Why not? It would be like Weight Watchers – once a week.'

'Leave me alone,' Shushu's voice was tired, withdrawn.

Kassim looked for Dina the next day at college and found her in the computer room. He sat on the swivel chair next to her and watched her as she worked. She was wearing glasses. He gave her the samosas he had made for her. Chicken and vegetable samosas in a greasy brown bag. Her gratitude and pleasure were the reward he wanted. She ate them straightaway even though there was a sign saying that no food or drink was allowed into the computer room.

✳ ✳ ✳

'I'm thinking of getting married,' Kassim said to Basheer. Five o'clock was quiet in the kebab shop. Things picked up after six and got brisker. The busiest time was when the pubs closed at eleven. 'That's great,' said Basheer. His eyes lit up as they did whenever he was deeply pleased.

'Still at the early stages,' said Kassim.

'*Inshallah* the wife you choose will be good and calm like you, and a strong believer,' he put his arm around Kassim.

'Thanks Basheer.'

'What for?'

'I've learnt a lot from you.'

Basheer shrugged and continued to hook alternate pieces of meat and green peppers onto a skewer.

Although Kassim regularly attended the converts' class at the mosque and learnt a lot, it was the daily contact with Basheer that had made him live Islam. It was working with Basheer, day-in day-out, through the mundane and the significant that had made Islam a rhythmic reality, a feasible way of living. Kassim had not had a religious upbringing. His Moroccan father had given him a Muslim name, circumcised him at the age of eight months, and took him to the children's mosque school only five times. After that, secular life had taken over. Kassim's Scottish mother had no interest in religion and no Muslim friends. She was close to her large Aberdeenshire family and Kassim grew up with Christmas and Hogmanay. Most times he felt he was just like his cousins, though he was conscious of his weird name and his father who spoke English with a funny accent. Kassim grew up a confident, happy child. Yet sometimes an incident would occur or someone would behave in a way that would make him stop, stand still and think, 'This canna be right.' He would not dwell on it too much, though. It was not in his nature to brood. Instead, he would shrug the feeling off and continue. It was judo that awakened his dormant Muslim identity. Judo lessons that were held in the city, away from his suburban home. He took the bus into town and his mother and cousins thought that judo was just a teenage whim that would pass. But he made friends with some of the other boys in the class. Arab boys who recognised his name straightaway.

Dina stood in front of the kebab shop and looked through the window. She could see Kassim cutting the doner kebab. He was wearing an apron. She watched him turn around to serve a customer, a tired-looking man with wispy hair combed over his balding forehead. Kassim sliced a loaf of pitta bread, put the doner kebab inside it. He held up a bottle of tahini. The man nodded. Kassim squeezed tahini into the sandwich. When the man shook his head at the offer of salad and hot sauce, Kassim put the sandwich into a brown paper bag. He wiped his hands on his apron, took a note from the man and opened the till. It was when he looked up, as the man was leaving, that he saw Dina. She saw his smile, surprised and happy to see her. It gave her this wide, good feeling that she associated with him; subconscious images of the sky rippling open, a healthy organ deep under the skin, succulence. He opened the door for her and said, '*Salamu alleikum*.'

It made her feel a bit self-conscious, this specifically Muslim greeting, new words she was not used to. She did not reply, only smiled and said, 'I was just passing by.'

Minutes later she was sitting down at one of the two tables that were in the shop. Kassim got her a piece of doner pizza, a samosa and an onion bhaji. He refused to let her pay. Samia came in with her baby in a pushchair. She remembered Dina and kissed her hello. Samia and Basheer spoke in loud Arabic, which Dina couldn't understand. Kassim interrupted them, 'Basheer, can I get a break, half an hour or so? I'll make it up later. Promise.'

When she finished eating, they went out for a walk. They walked along the beach. The sea was dark denim and sleek dolphins rose from the water and twisted back into it again. The wind blew Dina's hair and the smell of the sea raised her spirits. She became talkative and bright. When they sat down on the sand, she leaned and kissed Kassim on the cheek, ran her fingers through his hair and beard. She expected him to turn round and kiss her, but he blushed, and though he did not move away from her, she sensed him tense and so she was the one who moved away.

He mumbled something about marriage.

'Even to kiss?' Her voice was soft. A dog barked in the background and the cries of the seagulls were jarring and rude.

He didn't reply and she felt sorry for him in the way that people feel sorry for the crippled and the paralysed. It was a kind of pity that drew them apart rather than close.

* * *

'Someone's coming round to pick up clothes for the Syrian refugees. I'm going to give him Dad's things.'

Shushu didn't reply and poured herself another drink. Ever since they had installed the satellite dish and Shushu could see the Egyptian channel, she watched it all weekend. She enjoyed it thoroughly, even though it sometimes made her envious and homesick.

When Kassim came, Shushu was sulky and refused to

speak to him. She pressed the remote control and the room was drowned in the voice of the Lebanese singer Nancy Ajram. 'We can sit in the kitchen,' Dina said to Kassim.

They sat in the kitchen. Dina started to show him her father's clothes. She had washed them, ironed them and folded them up neatly. She had spent hours doing it, with Shushu sneering in the background.

Kassim started to tell her about Syria, about the hundreds of thousands killed, people losing their homes and living in camps. She started to cry and he thought she was moved by what he had been saying. But she had not really taken in what he was saying; it was all so far away. She cried for her father, she was, for the first time, freely grieving. Kassim, and what he was saying about Syria, took her away from her mother's bitterness, her mother's opinion of her father.

Gin made Shushu crave olives. Naughty olives that were full of calories. She resisted at first, then left the television to get the jar from the fridge. She discovered Dina sobbing and Kassim looking embarrassed.

'Why are you crying?' She turned to Kassim, 'You made her cry. Why is she crying? What did you do to upset her?'

'Nothing, Mrs McIntyre.'

'Then why is she crying?'

'Mum, I'm okay,' said Dina breathing. 'It's nothing. He didn't make me cry.'

'Why is he here anyway?' Shushu whispered under her breath, but it was audible. She got the jar of green olives out of the fridge and sat with them at the table.

'I'd better be off,' said Kassim standing up.

'See you.' Dina felt glued to her chair, heavy and unattractive.

'Yeah, see you.'

'Goodbye Mrs McIntyre.'

Shushu didn't answer and instead twisted open the jar of olives. Kassim picked up the black bin liner that was full of clothes and saw himself out, quietly closing the kitchen door.

Shushu dipped her fingers into brine and popped an olive in her mouth. Dina followed, then wiped her eyes with the back of her hand. 'I forgot to give him Dad's suits.'

For all her faults, Shushu had a mother's instinct. She sensed the threat of Kassim. 'So that's the boy from the kebab shop ...'

'I like him.' Dina bit into another olive. The green ones were always more bitter than the black.

'You'll end up in a horrible council flat with racist graffiti on the wall.' There was no menace in Shushu's voice, just disappointment.

They did not move until they had finished all the olives in the jar. Only the brine remained, wasted vinegar speckled green with bits of olive.

* * *

The bag of clothes was heavy and Kassim took the bus instead of walking. It did not take him long to get over the shock of Shushu. He had seen her type late at night in the kebab shop, women ravaged by dieting and trying too hard. He pitied them, as if they were ill or handicapped. It was the kind of pity that made them distant, far removed. If Kassim was given to irony he would have compared Dina's Muslim mother to his own Western mother and laughed. His mother was conservative and sedate, prim and house-proud. But Kassim was not given to irony or despair. He believed that wrong could be made right, nothing was impossible and things could improve.

By the time he reached the kebab shop and put the clothes at the back with all the other donations, going to Syria, he had forgotten all about Shushu. The rice he cooked that night was a success. There were congratulations from Basheer. 'You've done it, Kassim. Every grain of rice can't stand the touch of its brother.' They laughed and high fived.

* * *

The next day Dina took her father's suits to the kebab shop. She got a lift in a friend's car and chatted all the way proudly about Kassim, Syria and the clothes. The fact that her father's clothes were going to the Syrian refugees gave his death a profoundness it hadn't had before. In the kebab shop, Basheer was busy serving customers. It was the first time for Dina to say '*Salamu alleikum*'. The self-consciousness passed when Basheer replied. He saw the clothes she was carrying and said, 'Thank you, this is a big help. Give them to Kassim, he's in the back.'

She had never before walked through the 'Staff Only' door. The excitement of knowing she was going to see Kassim again, after a few steps, after a few minutes. And she was not an outsider today, not a customer, but one of 'them', pushing open a private door, as if she were Samia, as if she were part of the family too. It was dark and she paused until her eyes adjusted. She was in a narrow corridor. Stacks of soft drinks came into view, a pile of chairs, bulk-bought aluminium foil containers, plastic plates, paper napkins, bin liners. There were also piles of the things that were going to the refugees. Nappies, blankets, shoes, toys, tins of food and packets of pasta. She walked a few steps. Coats and jackets were hanging on a row of hooks that ran along the side of a wall. She found a free hook and hung up her father's suits. She heard a sneeze and said, 'Kassim?' But there was no reply. A small room, not much bigger than a wardrobe, opened out after the row of jackets. She heard a faint whisper and the rustle of movement and knew he was there. 'Kassim?'

It was then that her heart started beating, her blood turned cold, because he was not within arm's reach, because he was down on the ground, and it was a shock to see him like that, so still and grovelling, not searching for something that had fallen, not answering her. It was fear that she felt. And wanting him to reassure her, wanting the shock to go away. Why was he like that, his forehead, nose and hands pressed onto the floor, why …? He sat up and did not speak to her, did not acknowledge her presence. Descended though Dina was from generations of Muslims, she had never seen anyone praying. On television, yes, or a photo in a schoolbook, but not within arm's reach, not in the same room, not someone she knew, someone that she loved. When she understood, her pulse rate dulled back to normal, her fear turned to embarrassment. 'I'm sorry,' she mumbled and turned away. If she had accidentally pushed the toilet door open and found him sitting on the loo, she would have apologised in the same way. Like seeing Samia that day feeding her baby, the intimacy of it, something fleshy and vulnerable.

Dina stumbled out of the dim corridor to the bright light of the shop, customers milling round, barbecue smoke and the happy ring of the till. She walked out to the street, to the cold normality of traffic, high heels hitting the tarmac, cars parked on the road. She stood very still, her back to the kebab shop, her eyes glued to the tyre of a parked car, seeing nothing. He was inviting her to his faith, her faith really, because she had been born into it. He was passing it on silently by osmosis, and how painful and slow her awakening would be! If she now waited long enough, he would come out looking for her. If she went home, he would know that she was not keen on his lifestyle, did not want to change her own. She paused on the pavement, hesitating between the succulent mystic life he promised, and the peckish unfulfillment of her parent's home.

Expecting to Give

The sun tilts toward me but there is a cold wind. I can
see it through the window, bouncing the pink petals on
the trees. I spend the mornings in bed to put off that first
standing up which makes me nauseous. The doctor says I
should try eating a cracker before I get up, but it doesn't
work. I walk to the bathroom and I'm sick in the basin.
White froth and then with further retches, it turns smooth
and dark yellow, like cough medicine, only bitter. Then
back into bed, sweaty and hungry.

Saif's been away eight days and nine hours. He's not
due back until next week. I can't phone him unless there's
an emergency. They don't like personal phone calls on the
rigs and he's not allowed to take his mobile phone because
it's against the regulations. I'm floppy without him. He
is excited and confident about the baby while I wade

through the days. Tomorrow I go to my first ultrasound appointment at the hospital. Husband offshore, parents in another country, not a single friend to accompany me.

I thought pregnancy meant radiant skin and a stomach to be proud of. But I am barely showing and held back by waves of sleep; anxieties about the baby, about the birth, about the world I hear about on the news. Whenever Saif comes home we dwell on the changes in my body. Only a swell below my navel but my breasts are bigger. Sometimes they hurt, a dull pleasant ache, a gradual heaviness.

Hunger like I have never experienced. I stare at the ceiling and know that, if necessary, I can fight someone for food and I can rummage through garbage looking for titbits. It is something I did not know about myself. The baby is a parasite, the pregnancy book says, the baby will take from you all that he needs. Well, the baby seems to need eggs with ketchup, beans with ketchup, crisps with ketchup… so this is what a craving is, I realize, this passion for tomatoes, their redness and taste. Yesterday it was stale bread with ketchup, and when the bread ran out, just one spoonful after another.

This is the most difficult challenge, getting out of bed. Not getting up to vomit and coming back, but getting up to have a shower and dress. If I am going to cry it will be now, first thing in the morning, with the nausea in my chest and the day stretching out ahead.

It's not fair, is it, that Saif has taken me away from my career, my friends, my family and brought me here only to leave me and go offshore? But I am being irrational. It is his work and I should be supportive. I had walked into this marriage with eagerness, with eyes wide open. My parents were becoming stifling, my friends boring and my womb, fertile and unattended, was eager to flourish and enclose. I did not want to sink into my thirties, to reach the desperate stage and acquire that expectant, stalking look.

Saif was the nicest of them all, fresh and honest in an irresistible way. Marriage was a good move, coming here the right choice. It's not a raw deal; it's actually a good package. Yes, there is the bad weather, the loneliness when Saif goes offshore, but when he is here it is like a holiday, one honeymoon after the other. In the two weeks that he is onshore we stay up late, we have breakfast at lunchtime, we go to the cinema, we go out shopping. It is nice to be able to afford things, and not have to skimp and save. He is generous really, when he is freezing on the wretched rig working night shifts he keeps himself going by repeating, 'Think of the bonus, think of the baby, think of the bonus.' I have a lot to thank Allah for, instead of crying.

I bribe myself with breakfast so that I can get through the shower. I toast bread and make an omelette with feta cheese and the necessary tomatoes. I put more tomatoes than eggs, more tomatoes than cheese. It is mysterious this craving, too intense to be explained away by a need for Vitamin C. Even the pregnancy books are unsure. They say it is hormones that will only settle at fourteen weeks but that doesn't explain why I have suddenly gone off coffee and can't live without tomato juice.

The post brings more rejection letters. All the job applications I sent out when I first moved here are bouncing back. But do I have the audacity to turn up to an interview pregnant? These days I am sick or asleep, restless for a specific taste, hiding from toxic scents real and imaginary. I clean the bathroom with ordinary soap to avoid harsh detergents, in the supermarket I bypass certain rows.

I drive to the kebab shop for lunch. Driving is a triumph for me, a reminder that I am not completely helpless, completely housebound. It is a throwback to my past single life, the career woman with the little car, with somewhere to go, always busy. In another part of the world I had been a social worker. I identified children at risk and set up a programme to rehabilitate teenage drug addicts. I have to stop the car and vomit in a paper cup. Nothing comes out but white froth, my breakfast has fast disappeared. It is an empty stomach than makes me sick, though it is hard to believe. When I am full, the nausea goes away. But I am digesting too fast. I can hardly hold myself back between one meal and the next. Traffic whizzes past me. I wipe my mouth with tissues and stuff them in the paper cup. It suddenly feels too warm in the car, I open the window, indicate and drive out.

The smell of the shop pleases me. I need the large kebab sandwich, the salad soaked in chilli. I ask for ketchup too. Ketchup on the tomatoes, ketchup soaking the bread and the meat. It runs down the side of my mouth. A slim woman pushes her way through the door. It rattles so hard that most of us look up. Her deranged hair is streaked blonde, her nose bruised red; she is not steady on her feet. She stands at the door trembling. 'Marouf,' she hisses. 'Marouf.' The youngest of the staff, handsome enough for Bollywood, rushes to her side, tries to lead her by the arm out to the street. She holds her ground, 'You *lied* to me. You did ... You told me you'd be back, you told me ... Come home...' She's whining now and the rest of the staff arc hiding their sniggers.

Marouf's face is dark with embarrassment. He tilts his head and squeezes her arm. His voice is too low for me to hear his replies. She starts to hurl abuse at him, one *ek* sound after the other. When he tries to push her out the door she cuffs his face. This unsteadies her momentarily and he is able to dislodge her into the street. The door clinks behind them. I squeeze more ketchup onto my salad. I finish my sandwich and my drink. Marouf comes back in and his work mates taunt him in a language I don't understand. The ketchup has run all over my plate and I don't have a spoon to lap it all up.

No longer hungry, I feel fine. The fresh air is doing me good. I hurry past Starbucks; the merest whiff of coffee threatens a nausea attack. Strange that I used to malfunction without two black coffees a day. How to explain this sensitivity to smells? The foetus protecting itself from the dangers of coffee is a proposition but then, not every pregnant woman has the same response.

I walk into a mother and baby store and wish that it wasn't too early to buy maternity clothes. I touch the baby products. Soft yellows and blues and pinks. Cuddly toys, terry cloth, cots and bubble bath. I pick up a bottle of baby oil and breathe in the scent. It fills me with wellness, with innocence; baby sweetness and joy. The baby clothes for girls are nicer than the ones for boys. This time tomorrow, after the ultrasound, will I know if my baby is a he or a she? I can't *want* a boy or *want* a girl, it is already predetermined, it is already, thrillingly, too late. I am carrying a brand new creation, a beauty to cuddle, a precious name, a fresh personality whose steps I will share. Next to me a woman, about eight months pregnant, is looking at the plastic baths. Her stomach is like a basketball that had fallen once on her lap, her navel is inside out, protruding against her T-shirt. I feel like I am in primary school looking up in awe at one of the senior girls. I buy vitamins and a cream for stretch marks. I buy two new bras. Saif will want to check out the car seat and the stroller. He will revel in all the baby gadgets, locks and mobiles – I smile thinking we will come here together.

Outside, I find myself face to face with the woman from the kebab shop. This time she is pushing a toddler in a pushchair and staring into the shop window. The little boy's hair is so long that the fringe is almost covering his eyes. She must have left him outside the kebab shop, I realize. He must have been all alone on the pavement all the time she and Marouf were having their fight! The baby sits up straight, clutching his foot with one hand and a packet of crisps in the other. Some of it falls to the ground.

It is because of him that I speak to her. 'I saw you back at the kebab shop. Are you alright now?' I bend to smile at her son. He looks at me and makes a lovely *ga* sound, his own distinctive voice, his few teeth sitting lonely in their gums. I want to lift him up, to bathe him, to feed him, to teach him. I am yearning for my own baby and my silent invisible swell of a stomach is a solemn promise, the secret I am waiting to share. Beyond the fog of lethargy and nausea, after the heaviness and the pain, I will look down at an infant in my arms. She will be the centre of my life, she will be in focus, in colour and everything around her will be blurred, in black and white. I reach out to touch the toddler's hair. It is so pale that it is almost white. Surely he is too fair to be Marouf's. Surely. I am judging his mother now and as if she can read my mind, she withdraws, her face grim. Without a word, she yanks the pushchair so that the poor child is jerked back into his seat.

'Wait,' I say, but she just walks faster. I catch up with her and she is forced to stop. My words come out in a rush, 'You should give him a rusk or a piece of fruit, not this snack that is not even potatoes! Get him something good. He needs proper food to grow. And cut his fringe, he can barely see through it...'

'I don't need you interfering! Mind your own bloody business.' She pushes down on the handlebars so that the pushchair jerks up and comes down on my toes. I stand rooted to the pain as she flounces off. And because I haven't spoken to anyone for days, I feel sorry for myself. I wipe my tears and hobble to the car. I used to have a gaggle of friends and invitations to parties. At work others listened when I made presentations – I even had an assistant in my last few months before I resigned. In that other past life, I never craved tomatoes and I must have passed one hard-done-by mother after the other without turning a hair.

Saif is getting out of a taxi just as I am parking my car. It is such a surprise that I almost bump the curb and forget to undo my seat belt. 'Careful', he calls out as he lifts his rig bag from the boot and pays off the taxi. He is smiling and tousled like he always is when he first comes home, still with the noise of the machines ringing in his ears, the wobble of the platform, the stinging wind of the North Sea. Now he can put all this behind him and have everything he's been looking forward to. How perfect of him to be here today! I need the weight of his arms, his voice telling me off, his fingers rummaging through the things I just bought. I run into his arms. He explains that there's been a false alarm at the rig and non-essential staff for the ongoing operation were evacuated as a precaution. Lucky for me he was one of them. He is still in his rig coveralls and the smell of the oil pushes its way up my nose, black grease down my throat, fumes in my gullet. I move my face as a burp turns into a gag, into a retch.

'What's wrong?' He holds me but I twist away. I stagger

to the side of the road and aim my mouth at the nearest bushes. The ground is pink with fallen cherry blossoms. 'It's the smell,' I splutter. 'I'm sorry. It's not you. Don't be hurt.'

He is though, a little. It's in his voice when he says, 'We'll be together tomorrow at the hospital for the ultrasound.'

This does make me feel better. The nausea ebbs and I want to doze off, just for a short nap. Tomorrow, after the appointment, we can go for lunch in town. Pizza, this time. Pizza with extra tomatoes.

The Aromatherapist's Husband

She told him that Mother Teresa had visited her in a dream. Adam braced himself for the consequences. 'She wants me to work in her orphanage in Calcutta.' The steam from Elaine's green tea shimmered between them.

'We'll save up to get you there,' he replied. This was his style, to humour her and at the same time nudge her towards practicality. She had tears in her eyes now as she launched into a description of the dream. The feeling of being chosen, of having the ability to help others, of possessing a power, a gift. There were so many things Adam would rather save up for than trekking halfway across the world. It startled him that he could imagine her travelling without him.

He had always considered himself to be the perfect balance for Elaine. She would be up in the clouds or, more precisely, up in the attic, while he fixed the girls' swing in the garden or took the cat to the vet. Elaine was always on the move, not necessarily forward but sideways, up, across. She was a chess piece that made her own rules.

When they had first met at college, she was studying nutrition and he was doing metalwork. She talked all the time about books she'd read or programmes on the television about the supernatural. She didn't seem to notice that Adam was only half-listening, captivated by the movement of her lips, her energy that seemed to ignite and propel him.

His family didn't approve of her. They said that she was too different, but Adam didn't care. Their objections sounded irrelevant and too late. After the wedding, Elaine started teaching yoga in the local centre. Neither of her pregnancies deterred her. She opted for a natural birth each time and used essential oils to cope with the pain. Her interest in alternative medicine started then. Throughout the years she breastfed the girls, she was reading and studying for a long-distance aromatherapy qualification.

Adam was the one who converted the attic into a treatment room. He put shelves on the walls and carried up the special massage bed. In no time, Elaine managed to cram the whole wall with crystals, burners, jars and bottles. Her clients trooped up the stairs, ignoring Adam as he sat watching Disney DVDs with the girls. Elaine's business was picking up but she let the housework slide. Under Adam's bare feet, the carpet was gritty with cereal and crumbs.

'When was the last time you hoovered?' he called up to her. He was already opening the utility cupboard to get the vacuum cleaner.

She skipped down the stairs, her eyes bright and almost breathless. 'I saw an angel,' she said. 'A little angel flying past. He came to take a bad vibe away.'

The next weekend she went away to a meditation retreat. A month later she spent a whole week at a psychic fair and came back with a photo of her aura captured by a special camera. Adam stared at the red, yellow and green lights billowing around her familiar face. 'You look like a witch,' he said.

Elaine gave him a fierce look. 'I consulted a psychic. She told me I have the healing gift.'

'But you know that already,' he said. 'You've helped so many people.' She had helped him too, massaging the small of his back with lavender essence mixed with warm jojoba oil.

'There's more,' she said. 'The psychic said my healing guide is a Red Indian. And another is a Somali warrior.'

Adam snorted. 'You're wasting good money on these sessions. You need to focus on your work.'

'No, I need to learn to channel my energy and communicate with my guides. Then I would be able to read the forces surrounding my clients. I would be able to work *with* my guides.'

Geranium for PMT, petunia for a sluggish kidney, clary sage for mood swings. The scents of the oils hung around him. He could only shake them off when he got to work. He worked night-shifts as a welder. As he napped during the day, he would hear the new age music coming down from above him.

Another black cat loped around the house. Elaine made sure they ate only protein-rich cat food. For the family, she cooked wholesome, organic meals despite Adam's occasional protests. When he craved red meat, he had to go and sit alone in Burger King.

That summer she took the girls and disappeared for two weeks. Adam started to put on the weight she had shielded him from. He lost the daily blessing of the two little ones. Often he was worried but they came back tanned and healthy. He hugged the girls and watched Elaine move around the house dressed like a gypsy.

'We travelled with the fair,' she explained. 'From city to city. The weather was perfect. We picked strawberries and had picnics on the beach. These girls haven't watched television in all the time they were away!' She sounded like she was boasting.

Adam felt even more left out. 'Aren't you going to ask what I've been doing?'

She folded her arms across her chest and said in a flat voice, 'So what have you been up to?'

He deliberately went through his boring routine, hour after hour, day after day.

But she had had enough, 'You should have just come with us. Why didn't you?'

'Because you never asked me,' he shouted.

He had taken the night off work to be with her but she sat up in bed hugging her knees as if she was in pain, 'There is so much I want to do, so much I want to see. I should have been in India by now.'

'It's not practical. It never was. There's the girls to consider, the house...'

'You go on about the same things but I am ahead of you, Adam.' She rocked from side to side. 'I am so, so ahead of you now. This is exactly what Indigo said.'

'Who the hell is Indigo?'

'A psychic clairvoyant. Indigo has been able to communicate with the Spirit all her life through vision, hearing and scent. She can tune into clients with amazing accuracy. She said someone close to me is holding me back.'

'I've done nothing to hold you back. All I've ever done is support you.'

'She smelt you Adam! She smelt grease and oil.'

'This marriage is over, isn't it?' he said.

The next day Elaine propped up a *For Sale* sign in the garden. And everything followed quickly after that.

Coloured Lights

I cried a little as the bus started to fill up with people
on Charing Cross Road and passed the stone lions in
Trafalgar Square. Not proper crying with sobs and moans
but a few silly tears and water dribbling from my nose.
It was not the West Indian conductor who checked my
pass that day but a young boy who looked bored. The
West Indian conductor is very friendly with me; he tells
me I look like one of his daughters and that he wants to
visit the Sudan one day, to see Africa for the first time.
When I tell him of our bread queues and sugar coupons,
he looks embarrassed and turns to leave me to collect the
fares of other passengers. I was crying for Taha or maybe
because I was homesick, not only for my daughters or my
family but sick with longing for the heat, the sweat and the
water of the Nile. The English word 'homesick' is a good

one; we do not have exactly the same word in Arabic. In Arabic my state would have been described as 'yearning for the homeland' or the 'sorrow of alienation' and there is also truth in this. I was alienated from this place where darkness descended unnaturally at 4pm and people went about their business as if nothing had happened.

I was in a country which Taha had never visited and yet his memory was closer to me than it had been for years. Perhaps it was my new solitude, perhaps he came to me in dreams I could not recall. Or was my mind reeling from the newness surrounding me? I was in London on a one-year contract with the BBC World Service. Each day as I read the news in Arabic, my voice, cool and distant, reached my husband in Kuwait, and my parents who were looking after my daughters in Khartoum.

Now I was older than Taha had been when he died. At that time he was ten years older than me and like my other brothers he had humoured me and spoiled me. When he died, my mind bent a little and has never straightened since. How could a young mind absorb the sudden death of a brother on the day of his wedding? It seemed at first to be a ghastly mistake, but that was an illusion, a mirage. The Angel of Death makes no mistakes. He is a reliable servant who never fails to keep his appointment at the predetermined time and place. Taha had no premonition of his own death. He was fidgety, impatient, but not for that, not for the end coming so soon. It was too painful to think of what must have been his own shock, his own useless struggle against the inevitable. Nor did anyone else have foreknowledge. How could we, when we were steeped in wedding preparations and our house was full of relatives helping with the wedding meal?

From the misty windows I saw the words 'Gulf Air' written in Arabic and English on the doors of the airline's office and imagined myself one day buying a ticket to go to Hamid in Kuwait. It seemed that the fate of our generation is separation, from our country or our family. We are ready to go anywhere in search of the work we cannot find at home. Hamid says that there are many Sudanese in Kuwait and he hopes that in the next year or so the girls and I will join him. Every week, I talk to him on the telephone, long leisurely conversations. We run up huge telephone bills but seem to be unable to ration our talking. He tells me amusing stories of the emirs whose horses he cures. In Sudan, cattle die from starvation or disease all the time, cattle which are the livelihood of many people. But one of the country's few veterinary surgeons is away, working with animals whose purpose is only to amuse. Why? So that his daughters can have a good education, so that he can keep up with the latest research in his field. So that he can justify the years of his life spent in education by earning the salary he deserves. And I thought of Taha's short life and wondered.

In Regent Street, the conductor had to shake himself from his lethargy and prevent more people from boarding the bus. The progress of the bus was slow in contrast to the shoppers who swarmed around in the brightly lit streets. Every shop window boasted an innovative display and there were new decorative lights in addition to the street lights. Lights twined around the short trees on the pavements, on wires stretched across the street. Festive December lights. Blue, red, green lights, more elaborate than the crude strings of bulbs that we use in Khartoum to decorate the wedding house.

But the lights for Taha's wedding did not shine as they were meant to on that night. By the time night came he was already buried and we were mourning, not celebrating. Over the period of mourning, the wedding dinner was gradually eaten by visitors. The women indoors, sitting on mattresses spread on the floors, the men on wobbling metal chairs in a tent pitched in front of our house, the dust of the street under their feet. But they drank water and tea and not the sweet orange squash my mother and her friends had prepared by boiling small oranges with sugar. That went to a neighbour who was bold enough to enquire about it. Her children carried the sweet liquid from our house in large plastic bottles, their eyes bright, their lips moist with expectation.

When Taha died I felt raw and I remained transparent for a long time. Death had come so close to me that I was almost exhilarated; I could see clearly that not only life but the world is transient. But with time, my heart hardened and I became immersed in the cares of day-to-day life. I had become detached from this vulnerable feeling and it was good to recapture it now and grieve once again. Taha's life: I was not there for a large part of it but I remember the time he got engaged and my own secret feelings of jealousy towards his fiancée. Muddled feelings of admiration and a desire to please. She was a university student and to my young eyes she seemed so articulate and self-assured. I remember visiting her room in the university hostels while Taha waited for us outside by the gate, hands in his pockets, making patterns in the dust with his feet. Her room was lively, in disarray with clothes and shoes scattered about and colourful posters on the wall. It was full of chatting roommates and friends who kept coming in and out to eat the last biscuits in the open packet on the desk, borrow the prayer mat or dab their eyes with kohl from a silver flask. They scrutinised my face for any likeness to Taha, laughed at jokes I could not understand, while I sat nervously on the edge of a bed, smiling and unable to speak. Later with Taha we went to a concert in the football grounds where a group of students sang. I felt very moved by a song in the form of a letter written by a political prisoner to his mother. Taha's bride afterwards wrote the words out for me, humming the tune, looking radiant and Taha remarked on how elegant her handwriting was.

In the shop windows dummies posed, aloof strangers in the frenzied life of Oxford Street. Wools, rich silks and satin dresses. 'Taha, shall I wear tonight the pink or the green?' I asked him on the morning of the wedding. 'See,

I look like, like a watermelon in this green.' His room was an extension of the house where a veranda used to be, a window from the hall still looked into it, the door was made of shutters. He never slept in his room. In the early evening we all dragged our beds outdoors so that the sheets were cool when it was time to gaze up at the stars. If it rained Taha did not care, he covered his head with the sheet and continued to sleep. When the dust came thickly, I would shake his shoulder to wake him up to go indoors and he would shout at me to leave him alone. In the morning his hair would be covered with dust, sand in his ears, his eyelashes. He would sneeze and blame me for not insisting, for failing to get him to move inside.

He smiled at me in my green dress; his suitcase – half-filled – lay open on the floor; he leaned against the shutters, holding them shut with his weight. Through them filtered the hisses and smells of frying, the clinking of empty water glasses scented with incense and the thud of a hammer on a slab of ice, the angry splinters flying in the air, disintegrating, melting in surrender when they greeted the warm floor. Someone was calling him, an aunt cupped a hand round her mouth, tongue strong and dancing from side to side, she trilled the ululation, the joy cry. When others joined her the sound rose in waves to fill the whole house. Was it a tape or was it someone singing that silly song *Our Bridegroom like Honey*? Where can you ever find another like him?

To answer my question about the dress, he told me

words I knew to be absurd but wanted to believe. 'Tonight you will look more beautiful than the bride.' The bus headed north and we passed Regent's Park and the Central Mosque; all was peaceful and dark after the congestion of the shopping centre. I was glad that there were no more coloured lights, for they are cheerful but false. I had held others like them before in my hands, wiping the dust off each bulb and saying to Taha, 'How could you have taken them from the electrician when they were so dusty?' And he had helped me clean them with an orange cloth that he used for the car because he was in a hurry to set them up all around the outside of the house. I had teased him saying that the colours were not in an ordered pattern. We laughed together trying to make sense of their order, but they were random, chaotic. Then Hamid, who was his friend, arrived and said he would help him set them up. I asked Taha to get me a present from Nairobi, where he was going for his honeymoon, and Hamid had looked, directly at me, laughed in his easy way and said without hiding his envy, 'He is not going to have time to get you any presents.' At that time, Hamid and I were not even engaged and I felt shy from his words and walked away from his gaze.

It was the lights that killed Taha. The haphazard, worn strings of lights that had been hired out for years to house after wedding house. A bare live wire carelessly touched. A rushed drive to the hospital where I watched a stray cat twist and rub its thin body around the legs of our bridegroom's death bed. And in the crowded corridors, people squatted on the floor and the screams for Taha were absorbed by the dirty walls, the listless flies and the generous, who had space and tears for a stranger they had never met before.

My mother, always a believing woman, wailed and wept but did not pour dirt on her head or tear her clothes like some ignorant women do. She just kept saying again and again, 'I wish I never lived to see this day.' Perhaps Hamid had the greatest shock, for he was with Taha when he was setting up the lights. Later he told me that when they buried Taha he had stayed at the graveside after the other men had gone. He had prayed to strengthen his friend's soul at its crucial moment of questioning. The moment in the grave, in the interspace between death and eternity when the Angels ask the soul, 'Who is your lord?' and there must be no wavering in the reply, no saying 'I don't know.' The answer must come swiftly with confidence and it was for this assurance, in the middle of what must have been Taha's fear, that Hamid prayed.

I had been in London for nearly seven months and I told no one about Taha. I felt that it would sound distasteful or like a bad joke, but electricity had killed others in Khartoum too, though I did not know them personally. A young boy once urinated at the foot of a lamp light which had a base from which wires stuck out, exposed. A girl in my school was cleaning a fridge, squatting barefoot in a puddle of melted ice with the electric socket too close.

The girl's younger sister was in my class and the whole class, forty girls, went in the school bus to visit the family at home. On the way we sang songs as if we were on a school picnic and I cannot help but remember this day with pleasure.

With time, the relationship between my family and Taha's bride soured. Carefully prepared dishes ceased to pass between my mother and hers. In the two Eids, during which we celebrated in one the end of the fasting month of Ramadan and in the other the feast of sacrifice, our families no longer visited. Out of a sense of duty, my parents had proposed that she marry another of my brothers but she and her family refused. Instead she married one of her cousins who was not very educated, not as much as Taha at any rate. Sometimes, I would see her in the streets of Khartoum with her children and we would only greet each other if our eyes met.

In Taha's memory, my father built a small school in his home village on the Blue Nile. One classroom built of mud to teach young children to read and write. The best charity for the dead is something continuous that goes on yielding benefit over time. But like other schools it kept running into difficulties: no books, costly paper, poor attendance when children were sometimes kept at home to help their parents. Yet my father persevered and the school had become something of a hobby for him in his retirement. It is also a good excuse for him to travel frequently from the capital to the village and visit his old friends and family. What my mother did for Taha was more simple. She bought a *zeer*, a large clay pot and had it fastened to a tree in front of our house. The *zeer* held water, keeping it cool and it was covered by a round piece of wood on which stood a tin mug for drinking. Early in the morning, I would fill it with water from the fridge and throughout the day passers-by, hot and thirsty from the glaring sun, could drink, resting in the shade of the tree. In London, I came across the same idea, memorial benches placed in gardens and parks where people could rest. My mother would never believe that anyone would voluntarily sit in the sun but then she had never seen cold, dark evenings like these.

It was time for me to get off the bus as we had long passed Lords Cricket Grounds, Swiss Cottage and Golders Green. My stop was near the end of the route and there were only a few passengers left. After dropping me off, the bus would turn around to resume its cycle. My grief for Taha comes in cycles as well, over the years, rising and receding. Like the appearance of the West Indian conductor, it is transient and difficult to predict. Perhaps he will be on the bus tomorrow evening. 'Like them Christmas lights?' he will ask, and, grateful to see a familiar face amidst the alien darkness and cold, I will say, 'Yes, I admire the coloured lights.'

The Museum

At first, Shadia was afraid to ask him for his notes. The earring made her afraid. And the long, straight hair that he tied up with a rubber band. She had never seen a man with an earring and such long hair. But then, she had never known such cold, so much rain. His silver earring was the strangeness of the West, another culture shock. She stared at it during classes, her eyes straying from the white scribbles on the blackboard. Most times she could hardly understand anything. Only the notation was familiar. But how did it all fit together? How did this formula lead to this? Her ignorance and the impending exams were horrors she wanted to escape. His long hair, a dull colour between yellow and brown, different shades. It reminded her of a doll she had when she was young. She had spent hours combing that doll's hair, stroking it. She had longed for such straight hair. When she went to Paradise she would have hair like that. When she ran it would fly behind her; if she bent her head down it would fall over like silk and sweep the flowers on the grass. She watched his pony-tail move as he wrote and then looked up at the board. She pictured her doll, vivid suddenly after years, and felt sick that she was daydreaming in class, not learning a thing.

The first days of term, when the classes started for the MSc in Statistics, she was like someone tossed around by monstrous waves. Battered as she lost her way to the different lecture rooms, fumbled with the photocopying machine, could not find anything in the library. She could scarcely hear or eat or see. Her eyes bulged with fright, watered from the cold. The course required a certain background, a background she didn't have. So she floundered, she and the other African students, the two Turkish girls and the men from Brunei. As this congregation from the Third World whispered their anxieties in grim Scottish corridors, the girls in nervous giggles, Asafa, the short, round-faced Ethiopian, said in his grave voice, 'Last year, last year a Nigerian on this very same course committed suicide. Cut his wrists.'

Us and them, she thought. The ones who would do well, the ones who would crawl and sweat and barely pass. Two predetermined groups. Asafa, generous and wise (he was the oldest), leaned over and whispered to Shadia, 'The Spanish girl is good. Very good.' His eyes bulged redder than Shadia's. He cushioned his fears every night in the university pub; she only cried. Their countries were next door neighbours but he had never been to Sudan, and Shadia had never been to Ethiopia. 'But we meet in Aberdeen!' she had shrieked when this information was exchanged, giggling furiously. Collective fear had its euphoria.

'That boy Bryan,' said Asafa, 'is excellent.'

'The one with the earring?'

Asafa laughed and touched his own unadorned ear. 'The earring doesn't mean anything. He'll get the Distinction. He did his undergraduate here, got First Class Honours. That gives him an advantage. He knows all the lecturers, he knows the system.' So the idea occurred to her of asking Bryan for the notes of his graduate year. If she strengthened her background in stochastic processes and time series, she would be better able to cope with the new material they were bombarded with every day. She watched him to judge whether he was approachable. Next to the courteous Malaysian students, he was devoid of manners. He mumbled and slouched and did not speak with respect to the lecturers. He spoke to them as if they were his equals. And he did silly things. When he wanted to throw a piece of paper in the bin, he squashed it into a ball and, from where he was sitting, aimed it at the bin. If he missed, he muttered under his breath. She thought that he was immature. But he was the only one who was sailing through the course.

The glossy handbook for overseas students had

explained about the 'famous British reserve' and hinted that they should be grateful, things were worse further south, less 'hospitable'. In the cafeteria, drinking coffee with Asafa and the others, the picture of 'hospitable Scotland' was something different. Badr, the Malaysian, blinked and whispered, 'Yesterday our windows got smashed; my wife today is afraid to go out.'

'Thieves?' asked Shadia, her eyes wider than anyone else's. 'Racists,' said the Turkish girl, her lipstick chic, the word tripping out like silver, like ice.

Wisdom from Asafa, muted before the collective silence, 'These people think they own the world ...' and around them the aura of the dead Nigerian student. They were ashamed of that brother they had never seen. He had weakened, caved in. In the cafeteria, Bryan never sat with them. They never sat with him. He sat alone, sometimes reading the local paper. When Shadia walked in front of him he didn't smile. 'These people are strange ... One day they greet you, the next day they don't ...'

On Friday afternoon, as everyone was ready to leave the room after Linear Models, she gathered her courage and spoke to Bryan. He had spots on his chin and forehead, was taller than her, restless, as if he was in a hurry to go somewhere else. He put his calculator back in its case, his pen in his pocket. She asked him for his notes and behind his glasses, his blue eyes took on the blankest look she had ever seen in her life. What was all the surprise for? Did he think she was an insect? Was he surprised that she could speak?

A mumble for a reply, words strung together. So taken aback, he was. He pushed his chair back under the table with his foot.

'Pardon?'

He slowed down, separated each word, 'Ah'll have them for ye on Monday.'

'Thank you.' She spoke English better than him! How pathetic. The whole of him was pathetic. He wore the same shirt every blessed day. Grey stripes and white.

On the weekends, Shadia never went out of the halls and, unless someone telephoned long distance from home, she spoke to no one. There was time to remember Thursday nights in Khartoum, a wedding to go to with Fareed, driving in his red Mercedes. Or the club with her sisters. Sitting by the pool drinking lemonade with ice, the waiters all dressed in white. Sometimes people swam at night, dived in the water, dark like the sky above. Here, in this country's weekend of Saturday and Sunday, Shadia washed her clothes and her hair. Her hair depressed her. The damp weather made it frizz up after she straightened it with hot tongs. So she had given up and now wore it in a bun all the time, tightly pulled back away from her face, the curls held down by pins and Vaseline Tonic. She didn't like this style, her corrugated hair, and in the mirror her eyes looked too large. The mirror in the public bathroom at the end of the corridor had printed on it, 'This is the face of someone with HIV.' She had written about this mirror to her sister, something foreign and sensational like hail and cars driving on the left. But she hadn't written that the mirror made her feel as if she had left her looks behind in Khartoum.

* * *

On the weekends, she made a list of the money she had spent, the sterling enough to keep a family alive back home. Yet she might fail her exams after all that expense, go back home empty-handed, without a degree. Guilt was cold like the fog of this city. It came from everywhere. One day she forgot to pray in the morning. She reached the bus stop and then realised that she hadn't prayed. That morning folded out like the nightmare she sometimes had, of discovering that she had gone out into the street without any clothes.

In the evening, when she was staring at multidimensional scaling, the telephone in the hall rang. She ran to answer it. Fareed's cheerful greeting. 'Here, Shadia, Mama and the girls want to speak to you.' His mother's endearments, 'They say it's so cold where you are …'

Shadia was engaged to Fareed. Fareed was a package that came with the 7Up franchise, the paper factory, the big house he was building, his sisters and widowed mother. Shadia was going to marry them all. She was going to be happy and make her mother happy. Her mother deserved happiness after the misfortunes of her life. A husband who left her for another woman. Six girls to bring up, to

educate and marry off. People felt sorry for her mother. But your Lord is generous; each of the girls, it was often said, was lovelier than the other. They were clever too: dentist, pharmacist, architect, and all with the best of manners.

'We are just back from looking at the house,' Fareed's turn again to talk. 'It's coming along fine, they're putting the tiles down...'

'That's good, that's good,' her voice strange from not talking to anyone all day.

'... the bathroom suites. If I get them all the same colour for us and the girls and Mama, I could get them on a discount. Blue, the girls are in favour of blue,' his voice echoed from one continent to another. Miles and miles.

'Blue is nice. Yes, better get them all the same colour.' He was building a block of flats, not a house. The ground-floor flat for his mother and the girls until they married, the first floor for him and Shadia. The girls' flats on the two top floors would be rented out.

When Shadia had first got engaged to Fareed, he was the son of a rich man. A man with the franchise for 7Up, and the paper factory which had a monopoly in ladies' sanitary towels. Fareed's sisters never had to buy sanitary towels and their house was abundant with boxes of Pinky, fresh from the production line. But Fareed's father died of an unexpected heart attack soon after the engagement party, an extravagant affair at the Hilton. Now Shadia was going to marry the rich man himself. 'You are a lucky, lucky girl,' her mother said, and Shadia rubbed soap in her

eyes so that Fareed would think she had been weeping his father's death.

There was no time to talk about her course on the telephone, no space for her anxieties. Fareed was not interested in her studies. He had said, 'I am very broad-minded to allow you to study abroad. Other men would not have put up with this…' It was her mother who was keen for her to study, to get a post-graduate degree from Britain and then have a career after she got married. 'This way,' her mother had said, 'you will have your in-laws' respect. They have money but you will have a degree. Don't end up like me. I left my education to marry your father and now…'

Many conversations ended bitterly, with her mother saying, 'No one suffers like I suffer,' making Shadia droop. At night her mother sobbed in her sleep, noises that woke Shadia and her sisters.

No, on the long-distance line, there was no space for her worries. Talk about the Scottish weather. Picture Fareed, generously perspiring, his stomach straining the buttons of his shirt. Often she had nagged him to lose weight with no success. His mother's food was too good – his sisters were both overweight. On the long-distance line, listen to the Khartoum gossip as if listening to a radio play.

* * *

On Monday, without saying anything, Bryan slid two folders across the table towards her as if he did not want to come near her, did not want to talk to her. She wanted to say, 'I won't take them till you hand them to me politely.' But smarting, she said, 'Thank you very much.' She had manners. She was well brought up.

Back in her room, at her desk, the clearest handwriting she had ever seen. Sparse on the pages, clean. Clear and rounded like a child's, the tidiest notes. She cried over them, wept for no reason. She cried until she wetted one of the pages, stained the ink, blurred one of the formulas. She dabbed at it with a tissue but the paper flaked and became transparent. Should she apologise about the stain? Say that she was drinking water, say that it was rain? Or should she just keep quiet and hope he wouldn't notice? She chided herself for all that worry. He wasn't concerned about wearing the same shirt every day. She was giving him too much attention thinking about him. He was just an immature and closed-in sort of character. He probably came from a small town; his parents were probably poor, low class. In Khartoum, she never mixed with people like that. Her mother liked her to be friends with people who were higher up. How else were she and her sisters going to marry well? She must study the notes and stop crying over this boy's handwriting. His handwriting had nothing to do with her, nothing to do with her at all.

Understanding after not understanding is fog lifting, is pictures swinging into focus, missing pieces slotting into place. It is fragments gelling, a sound vivid whole, a basis to build on. His notes were the knowledge she needed, the gaps. She struggled through them, not skimming them with the carelessness of incomprehension, but taking them in, making them a part of her, until in the depth of concentration, in the late hours of the nights, she lost awareness of time and place and at last when she slept she became epsilon and gamma and she became a variable making her way through discrete space from state i to state j.

* * *

It felt natural to talk to him. As if now that she had spent hours and days with his handwriting, she knew him in some way. She forgot the offence she had taken when he had slid his folders across the table to her, all the times he didn't say hello.

In the computer room, at the end of the statistical packages class, she went to him and said, 'Thanks for the notes. They are really good. I think I might not fail, after all. I might have a chance to pass.' Her eyes were dry from all the nights she had stayed up. She was tired and grateful.

He nodded and they spoke a little about the Poisson distribution, Queuing theory. Everything was clear in his mind, his brain was a transparent pane of glass where all the concepts were written out boldly and neatly. Today, he seemed more at ease talking to her, though he still shifted about from foot to foot, avoided her eyes.

He said, 'Do ye want to go for a coffee?'

She looked up at him. He was tall and she was not used to speaking to people with blue eyes. Then she made a mistake. Perhaps because she had been up late last night, she made that mistake. Perhaps there were other reasons for that mistake. The mistake of shifting from one level to another.

She said, 'I don't like your earring.'

The expression in his eyes was new, a focusing, no longer shifting away. He lifted his hand to his ear and tugged the earring off. His earlobe without the silver looked red and scarred.

She giggled because she was afraid, because he wasn't smiling, wasn't saying anything. She covered her mouth with her hand then wiped her forehead and eyes. A mistake was made and it was too late to go back. She plunged ahead, careless now, reckless, 'I don't like your long hair.'

He turned and walked away.

* * *

The next morning, Multivariate Analysis, and she came in late, dishevelled from running in the rain. The professor, whose name she wasn't sure of (there were three who were Mc something), smiled unperturbed. All the lecturers were relaxed and urbane, in tweed jackets and polished shoes.

Sometimes she wondered how the incoherent Bryan, if he did pursue an academic career, was going to transform himself into a professor like that. But it was none of her business.

Like most of the other students, she sat in the same seat in every class. Bryan sat a row ahead which was why she could always look at his hair. But he had cut it – there was no ponytail today! Just his neck and the collar of the grey and white-striped shirt.

Notes to take down. *In discriminant analysis, a linear combination of variables serves as the basis for assigning cases to groups ...*

She was made up of layers. Somewhere inside, deep under the crust of vanity, in the untampered-with essence, she would glow and feel humbled, thinking, this is just for me, he cut his hair for me. But there were other layers, bolder, more to the surface. Giggling. Wanting to catch hold of a friend. Guess what? You wouldn't believe what this idiot did!

Find a weighted average of variables ... The weights are estimated so that they result in the best separation between the groups.

After the class he came over and said very seriously, without a smile, 'Ah've cut my hair.'

A part of her hollered with laughter, sang, you stupid boy, you stupid boy, I can see that, can't I?

She said, 'It looks nice.' She said the wrong thing and her face felt hot and she made herself look away so that she would not know his reaction. It was true though, he did look nice, he looked decent now.

* * *

She should have said to Bryan, when they first held their coffee mugs in their hands and were searching for an empty table, 'Let's sit with Asafa and the others.' Mistakes follow mistakes. Across the cafeteria, the Turkish girl saw them together and raised her perfect eyebrows; Badr met Shadia's eyes and quickly looked away. Shadia looked at Bryan and he was different, different without the earring and the ponytail, transformed in some way. If he would put lemon juice on his spots ... but it was none of her business. Maybe the boys who smashed Badr's windows looked like Bryan, but with fiercer eyes, no glasses. She must push him away from her. She must make him dislike her.

He asked her where she came from and when she replied, he said, 'Where's that?'

'Africa,' with sarcasm. 'Do you know where that is?'

His nose and cheeks under the rim of his glasses went red.

Good, she thought, good. He will leave me now in peace.

He said, 'Ah know Sudan is in Africa. Ah meant where exactly in Africa.'

'North-east, south of Egypt. Where are you from?'

'Peterhead. It's north of here. By the sea.'

It was hard to believe that there was anything north of Aberdeen. It seemed to her that they were on the northern-most corner of the world. She knew better now than to imagine sun-tanning and sandy beaches for his 'by the sea'. More likely it was dismal skies and pale, bad-tempered people shivering on the rocky shore.

'Your father works in Peterhead?'

'Aye, he does.'

She had grown up listening to the proper English of the BBC World Service only to come to Britain and find people saying 'yes' like it was said back home in Arabic, *aye*.

'What does he do, your father?'

He looked surprised, his blue eyes surprised, 'Ma' dad's a joiner.'

Fareed hired people like that to work on the house. Ordered them about.

'And your mother?' she asked.

He paused a little, stirred sugar in his coffee with a plastic spoon. 'She's a lollipop lady.'

Shadia smirked into her coffee, took a sip.

'My father,' she said proudly, 'is a doctor, a specialist.' Her father was a gynaecologist. The woman who was his wife now had been one of his patients. Before that, Shadia's friends had teased her about her father's job, crude jokes that made her laugh. It was all so sordid now.

'And my mother,' she blew the truth up out of proportion, 'comes from a very big family. A ruling family.

If you British hadn't colonised us, my mother would have been a princess now.'

'Ye walk like a princess,' he said.

What a gullible, silly boy! She wiped her forehead with her hand, said, 'You mean I am conceited and proud?'

'No, ah didnae mean that, no…' The packet of sugar he was tearing open tipped from his hand, its contents scattering over the table. 'Ah shit … sorry …' He tried to scoop up the sugar and knocked against his coffee mug, spilling a little on the table.

She took out a tissue from her bag, reached over and mopped up the stain. It was easy to pick up all the bits of sugar with the damp tissue.

'Thanks,' he mumbled and they were silent. The cafeteria was busy, full of the humming, buzzing sounds of people talking to each other, trays and dishes. In Khartoum, she avoided being alone with Fareed. She preferred it when they were with others, their families or their many mutual friends. If they were ever alone, she imagined that her mother was with them, could hear them, and spoke to Fareed with that audience in mind.

Bryan was speaking to her, saying something about rowing on the river Dee. He belonged to a rowing club and went rowing on the weekends.

To make herself pleasing to people was a skill Shadia was well-trained in. It was not difficult to please people. Agree with them, never dominate the conversation, be economical with the truth. Now here was someone whom all these rules needn't apply to. She said to him, 'The Nile is superior to the Dee. I saw your Dee, it is nothing, it is like a stream. There are two Niles, the Blue and the White, named after their colours. They come from the south, from two different places. They travel for miles, over countries with different names, never knowing they will meet. I think they get tired of running alone, it is such a long way to the sea. They want to reach the sea so that they can rest, stop running. There is a bridge in Khartoum and under this bridge the two Niles meet, and if you stand on the bridge and look down, you can see the two waters mixing together.'

'Do ye get homesick?' he asked and she felt tired now, all this talk of the river running to rest in the sea. She had never talked like that before.

'Things I should miss I don't miss. Instead I miss things I didn't think I would miss. The *azan*, the Muslim call to prayer from the mosque, I don't know if you know about it. I miss that. At dawn it used to wake me up. I would hear 'prayer is better than sleep' and just go back to sleep – I never got up to pray.' She looked down at her hands on the table. There was no relief in confessions, only his smile, young, with something like wonder in his eyes.

'We did Islam in school,' he said. 'Ah went on a trip to Mecca.' He opened out his palms on the table.

'What!'

'In a book.'

'Oh.'

The coffee was finished. They should go now. She should go to the library before the next lecture and photocopy previous exam papers. Asafa, full of helpful advice, had shown her where to find them.

'What is your religion?' she asked.

'Dunno, nothing ah suppose.'

'That's terrible! That's really terrible!' Her voice was too loud, too concerned.

His face went red again and he tapped his spoon against the empty mug.

Waive all politeness, make him dislike her. Badr had said, even before his windows got smashed, that here in the West they hate Islam. Standing up to go, she said flippantly, 'Why don't you become a Muslim then?'

He shrugged, 'Ah wouldnae mind travelling to Mecca; ah was keen on that book.'

Her eyes filled with tears. They blurred his face when he stood up. In the West they hate Islam and he... She said, 'Thanks for the coffee' and walked away. He followed her.

'Shadiya, Shadiya,' he pronounced her name wrong, three syllables instead of two, 'there's this museum about Africa. I've never been before. If you'd care to go, tomorrow...'

* * *

No sleep for the guilty, no rest. She should have said no, I can't go, no I have too much catching up to do. No sleep for the guilty, the memories come from another continent. Her father's new wife, happier than her mother, fewer worries. When Shadia visits, she offers fruit in a glass bowl, icy oranges and guava, soothing in the heat. Shadia's father hadn't wanted a divorce, hadn't wanted to leave them – he wanted two wives, not a divorce. But her mother had too much pride, she came from fading money, a family with a 'name'. Of the new wife, her mother says, 'bitch', 'whore', 'the dregs of the earth', 'a nobody'.

Tomorrow, she need not show up at the museum, even though she said that she would. She should have told Bryan that she was engaged to be married, mentioned it casually. What did he expect from her? Europeans had different rules, reduced, abrupt customs. If Fareed knew about this... her secret thoughts like snakes... Perhaps she was like her father, a traitor. Her mother said that her father was devious. Sometimes Shadia was devious. With Fareed in the car, she would deliberately say, 'I need to stop at the grocer, we need things at home.' At the grocer he would pay for all her shopping and she would say, 'No, you shouldn't do that, no, you are too generous, you are embarrassing me.' With the money she saved, she would buy a blouse for her mother, nail varnish for her mother, a magazine, imported apples.

* * *

It was strange to leave her desk, lock her room and go out on a Saturday. In the hall, the telephone rang. It was Fareed. If he knew where she was going now... Guilt was like a hard-boiled egg stuck in her chest. A large, cold egg.

'Shadia, I want you to buy some of the fixtures for the bathrooms. Taps and towel hangers. I'm going to send you a list of what I want exactly and the money...'

'I can't, I can't.'

'What do you mean you can't? If you go into any large department store...'

'I can't. I wouldn't know where to put these things, how to send them.'

There was a rustle on the line and she could hear someone whispering, Fareed distracted a little. He would be at work at this time of day, glass bottles filling up with clear effervescence, '7Up' written in English and Arabic, white against the dark green.

'You can get good things, things that aren't available here. Gold would be good. It would match...'

Gold. Gold toilet seats!

'People are going to burn in Hell for eating out of gold dishes; you want to sit on gold!'

He laughed. He was used to getting his own way, not easily threatened, 'Are you joking with me?'

'No.'

In a quieter voice, 'This call is costing...'

She knew, she knew. He shouldn't have let her go away. She was not coping with the whole thing, she was not handling the stress. Like the Nigerian student.

'Shadia, gold-coloured, not gold. It's smart.'

'Allah is going to punish us for this; it's not right...'

'Since when have you become so religious!'

Bryan was waiting for her on the steps of the museum, familiar-looking against the strange grey of the city, streets where cars had their headlamps on in the middle of the afternoon. He wore a different shirt, a navy-blue jacket. He said, not looking at her, 'Ah was beginning to think you wouldnae turn up.'

There was no entry fee to the museum, no attendant handing out tickets. Bryan and Shadia walked on soft carpets, thick blue carpets that made Shadia want to take off her shoes. The first thing they saw was a Scottish man from Victorian times. He sat on a chair surrounded with possessions from Africa, over-flowing trunks, an ancient map strewn on the floor of the glass cabinet. All the light in the room came from this and other glass cabinets, gleamed on the wax. Shadia turned away; there was an ugliness in the life-like wispiness of his hair, his determined expression, the way he sat. A hero who had gone away and come back, laden with looted treasures, ready to report.

Bryan began to conscientiously study every display cabinet, read the posters on the wall. She followed him around and thought that he was studious, careful and studious, that was why he did so well in his degree. She watched the intent expression on his face as he looked at everything. For her the posters were an effort to read, the information difficult to take in. It had been so long since she had read anything outside the requirements of the course. But she persevered, saying the words to herself, moving her lips ... *During the eighteenth and nineteenth centuries, north-east Scotland made a disproportionate impact on the world at large by contributing so many skilled and committed individuals... In serving an empire they gave and received, changed others and were themselves changed and often returned home with tangible reminders of their experiences.*

The tangible reminders were there to see, preserved in spite of the years. Her eyes skimmed over the objects, disconnected from place and time. Iron and copper, little statues. Nothing was of her, nothing belonged to her life at home, what she missed. Here was Europe's vision, the clichés about Africa: cold and old.

She had not expected the dim light and the hushed silence. Apart from Shadia and Bryan, there was only a man with a briefcase and a lady who took down notes. Unless there were others, out of sight on the second floor. Something electrical, the heating or the lights, gave out a humming sound like that of an air-conditioner. It made Shadia feel as if they were in an airplane without windows, detached from the world outside.

'He looks like you, don't you think?' she said to Bryan. They stood in front of a portrait of a soldier who died in the first year of this century. It was the colour of his eyes and his hair. But Bryan did not answer her, did not agree with her.

He was preoccupied with reading the caption. When she looked at the portrait again, she saw that she was mistaken. That strength in the eyes, the purpose, was something Bryan didn't have. They had strong faith in those days long ago.

Biographies of explorers who were educated in Edinburgh. They knew what to take to Africa: Christianity, commerce, civilisation. They knew what they wanted to bring back: cotton watered by the Blue Nile, the Zambezi river. She walked after Bryan, felt his concentration, his interest in what was before him and thought, in a photograph we would not look nice together.

She touched the glass of a cabinet showing papyrus rolls and copper pots. She pressed her forehead and nose against the cool glass. If she could enter the cabinet, she would not make a good exhibit. She wasn't right; she was too modern, too full of mathematics.

Only the carpet, its petroleum blue, pleased her. She had come to this museum expecting sunlight and photographs of the Nile, something to appease her homesickness, a comfort, a message. But the messages were not for her, not for anyone like her. A letter from West Africa, 1762, an employee to his employer in Scotland. An employee trading European goods for African curiosities. *It was a great difficulty to make the natives understand my meaning, even by an interpreter, it being a thing so seldom asked of them, but they have all undertaken to bring something and laughed heartily at me and said, I was a good man to love their country so much...*

Love my country so much. She should not be here; there was nothing for her here. She wanted to see minarets, boats fragile on the Nile, people. People like her father. Times she had sat in the waiting room of his clinic, among pregnant women, the pain in her heart because she was going to see him in a few minutes. His room, the air-conditioner, the smell of his pipe, his white coat. When she hugged him, he smelled of Listerine mouthwash. He could never remember how old she was, what she was studying. Six daughters, how could he possibly keep track? In his confusion, there was freedom for her, games to play, a lot of teasing. She visited his clinic in secret, telling lies to her mother. She loved him more than she loved her mother. Her mother who did everything for her, tidied her room, sewed her clothes from *Burda* magazine. Shadia was twenty-five and her mother washed everything for her by hand, even her pants and bras.

'I know why they went away,' said Bryan. 'I understand why they travelled.' At last he was talking. She had not seen him this intense before. He spoke in a low voice, 'They had to get away, to leave here...'

'To escape from the horrible weather...' She was making fun of him. She wanted to put him down. The imperialists who had humiliated her history were heroes in his eyes.

He looked at her. 'To escape...' he repeated.

'They went to benefit themselves,' she said. 'People go away because they benefit in some way...'

'I want to get away,' he said.

She remembered when he had opened his palms on the table and said, 'I went on a trip to Mecca.' There had been pride in his voice.

'I should have gone somewhere else for the course,' he went on. 'A new place, somewhere down south.'

He was on a plateau, not like her. She was punching and struggling for a piece of paper that would say she was awarded an MSc from a British university. For him, the course was a continuation.

'Come and see,' he said, and he held her arm. No one had touched her before, not since she had hugged her mother goodbye. Months now in this country and no one had touched her.

She pulled her arm away. She walked away, quickly up the stairs. Metal steps rattled under her feet. She ran up the stairs to the next floor. Guns, a row of guns aiming at her. They had been waiting to blow her away. Scottish arms of centuries ago, gunfire in service of the empire.

Silver muzzles, now a dirty grey. They must have shone pretty once, under a sun far away. If they blew her away now, where would she fly and fall? A window that looked out at the hostile sky. She shivered despite the wool she was wearing, despite the layers of clothes. Hell is not only blazing fire – a part of it is freezing cold, torturous ice and snow. In Scotland's winter you live a glimpse of this unseen world, feel the breath of it in your bones.

There was a bench and she sat down. There was no one

here on this floor. She was alone with sketches of jungle animals, words on the wall. A diplomat away from home, in Ethiopia in 1903, Asafa's country long before Asafa was born. *It is difficult to imagine anything more satisfactory or better worth taking part in than a lion drive. We rode back to camp feeling very well indeed. Archie was quite right when he said that this was the first time since we have started that we have really been in Africa – the real Africa of jungle inhabited only by game, and plains where herds of antelope meet your eye in every direction.*

'Shadiya, don't cry.' He still pronounced her name wrong because she had not shown him how to say it properly.

He sat next to her on the bench, the blur of his navy jacket blocking the guns and the wall-length pattern of antelope herds. She should explain that she cried easily, that there was no need for the alarm on his face. His awkward voice, 'Why are ye crying?' He didn't know, he didn't understand. He was all wrong, not a substitute...

'They are telling you lies in this museum,' she said. 'Don't believe them. It's all wrong. It's not jungles and antelopes, it's people. We have things like computers and cars. We have 7Up in Africa and some people, a few people, have bathrooms with golden taps... I shouldn't be here with you. You shouldn't talk to me...'

He said, 'Museums change; I can change...'

He didn't know it was a steep path she had no strength for. He didn't understand. Many things, years and landscapes, gulfs. If she was strong, she would have explained and not tired of explaining. She would have patiently taught him another language, letters curved like the epsilon and gamma he knew from mathematics. She would have shown him that words could be read from right to left. If she was not small in the museum, if she was really strong, she would have made his trip to Mecca real, not only in a book.

The Circle Line

Cheese melts in London like nowhere else. Old mixes with new like nowhere else. The city is blessed. But a girl can sob her heart out in London's streets and no one will stop, no one will raise an eyebrow, no one will ask why. Oh, city of opportunities, career ladders and fame, you promised me I could start afresh, make my fortune. Rise and cruise up high. But I age and watch the chances fold in, the paths converge. I live the narrowing and the shutting down.

This shrinkage makes for a modest life, a failure. It opens the trapdoor on what I thought was beneath me: the cesspool of bitter and delirious crime. Last year my fiancé was arrested for money laundering. I had no inkling of it, not the vaguest idea. Lucky you didn't go down with him, people tell me. They can't be bothered with the state of my heart.

After I broke off with him, my mother took to sending me alternative suitors. It is easier to meet them here in London. In Abu Dhabi we would have to be chaperoned, or at least pretend to be. Here we can be alone. Here it's all quicker: from the awkward first meeting to seeing through the veneer of appearances, nurturing a spark, aborting a project before it becomes formal. Here we are allowed a more organic start.

I wake to the buzz of a message from her. We Skype while I eat my toast. She is three hours ahead of me and chirpy. 'After our last tragic experience, we need to stick to families that we know.'

It is nice of her to say 'our' to include herself in my disgrace. But it could also be a ploy to soften me. I know her tricks. She goes on, with confidence, 'Remember Hisham, the son of Dr Suad? You must remember him from that time we met up in Alexandria. How old were you then? Thirteen or fourteen? I gave him your number. He is only in London for a few days. You must meet up.'

I flick back two decades to a snapshot of Hisham, skinny in a navy swimsuit and poking at a patch of seaweed. He is saying, 'It's edible! It's edible!' No one else shares his excitement. At the age of fourteen, I already knew about crushes, I knew who I fancied and who I didn't. At the age of fourteen, I assessed Hisham and concluded that he was not my type.

'I'm busy,' I say to my mother.

'You are thirty-four.'

'Thirty-three.' My birthday is in November.

Her mood changes, 'In a few years' time, the situation will no longer be a joke.'

I have heard this lecture time and time again. Years flying, fertility falling; how I'm becoming more and more set in my ways, how no man is perfect. 'So what is the catch with this one?' I ask. These suitors always have a defect. The first one she sent was too short; the second only spoke to say that he hated London and the third should have been right – three is a good number, after all – but he confessed that his family had put pressure on him to meet me while he was actually in love with another girl, unsuitable no doubt. The fourth was too religious.

'You,' my mother sighs. 'You are the only obstacle.'

* * *

He phones me as I step into Hyde Park. Before I break into my after-work jog and start to breathe heavily. It's sunny today. Girls stretch out on the grass, their lipstick melting in the sun. I stride past ghetto blasters and smelly dogs, tepid ice cream handed down to children. Hisham tells me he's staying in a hotel in Bayswater. He's left the NGO with which he'd spent eighteen months in Darfur. In a few days' time, he will take the train to Edinburgh to visit his brother who is studying there.

'I'm giving private Arabic lessons in the evenings,' I say. 'It's amazing how many people now want to learn. And they're willing to pay well for it!'

He laughs and says that sounds good, that sounds interesting. I stand still and look at the playground. An overweight Arab boy is panting over the sand pit. His Filipino nanny stands over him, her skinny arms on her hips. This job has taken her from her lush homeland, through Doha or Bahrain. For a few months she will walk London's tired grass. In holiday photos and video clips, she will be an exotic flower in the background.

'I am sorry to hear about your broken engagement,' he is saying.

I mumble something in reply.

Hisham's voice sounds distant as if he is looking away, 'The need for money can make the throat go tight. But some people have neither morals nor restraint.'

The last thing I want is to discuss my ex. So I make my voice light, 'You've become a philosopher, Hisham.'

'Yes. And I'm intrigued by the Circle Line – by all things that are inaccurately named.'

'Pardon?'

'In the Underground. I took the Circle Line and it didn't bring me back where I started. Apparently the trains no longer run a continuous circle. Instead they travel in a semicircle and there are now actually two routes.'

I remember now, this quirkiness of his. How he was sometimes geeky, sometimes soulful. How he earnestly revealed information, things he must have read about or remembered from TV. 'Merlin is a kind of falcon. The Nile is the longest river. Seaweed is edible.' Now he wants me to show him around London.

We agree to meet up tomorrow; perhaps it won't be as hot as today. It is at this time of year that I miss Abu Dhabi the most. I miss the spacious malls and the blast of the air conditioners. Here, it is as if the sun of the Empire has come to pay respect. London swells with planeloads of tourists. Tourists with big appetites, cash heavy, mouths watering, eyes popping.

'Bloody foreigners!' screeches a harassed mother as they stampede her and her infant, getting on a bus in Oxford Street. 'Every bloody summer.'

The buses are full of women. Women with pushchairs and little old women, shaking away. Dreamy schoolgirls stalked by bullies. The slow red buses are dignified like the Queen.

City of generous absorption, of waddling matrons in black abayas and face veils consulting Harley Street specialists, of sulky adolescents seeking distraction in Madame Tussauds. Ancient Egypt's gold, lying cold in a museum. The tennis at Wimbledon, the pigeons in Trafalgar Square. And an order, a fairness; an obligation to make things better even in some little way. Under Marble Arch I feel the weight of history.

In the streets: nose rings, dreadlocks, skinheads, pin dug through an eyebrow, man dressed as woman, dog dressed as man, a placard raised high – *Jesus Is Coming*.

But this is also a city of fashion. Nearly everyone

looks good in London. It's the hair and the new clothes. Londoners make an effort, having faith in the pages of glossy magazines. Or else it's turbans and saris: Nigerian women in paradise greens and head wraps so large only they could carry them.

Down in the Underground station it is warmer. I wonder what Hisham will be like after all these years. I wonder why I never looked him up on Facebook. Jubilee line, Metropolitan line. Crystal Palace and Marble Arch. What will I tell him about the Circle Line, and how Oxford Circus is not a circus?

He can't truly know London until he is here in winter with its fog and gloves and Christmas lights. There are secrets, then, under the dark coats and bare trees. In the wisps of smoke from breath and street lights. It is also important to know that in Speakers' Corner, not everyone is insane. Not everyone.

* * *

We meet off Regent Street in a café with pictures of dead Hollywood stars, and an American slant to the menu. Ten in the morning and it feels early for London. Clean, not too much traffic, not too much heat.

A sudden sticky nostalgia when I first see him. His shoulders are broader, his hair is cut short. I briefly crave the frenzy of our younger selves, itchy swimsuits and sunburn, the blast of the sea, our parents in the background, genial and laughing. What if I never have children? Hisham orders a cappuccino and I order an iced Coffee Extravaganza, trying it for the first time. It comes tall and sweet, sealed at the top with thick white cream. It tastes so good, I can't believe it.

'Have another one,' he says. I am shocked at this suggestion, intrigued. I say no. It will be greedy, all that ice and cream.

The second glass lasts longer. I sip through the straw and there is caramel at the bottom. 'There's caramel at the bottom,' I say, and offer him some. He shakes his head.

I was four when my parents moved to Abu Dhabi. Flushed with new money, they fed me on McDonalds and Pizza Hut, indulged me until I refused to eat anything else. I ate nothing but junk food for two years until I fell ill. It was a struggle to wean me off it, get me to eat a solid meal. For a long time anything green felt strange and tickly in my mouth.

'How long will you keep hiding in London?' he asks.

I am taken aback and launch into a long and hectic explanation. I brag about how regularly I jog in the park and about the new car I am buying. He must never feel sorry for me.

He says he's burnt out after eighteen months in Darfur. He says he can't talk about what it was like in the camps. He spreads his palms out to take in our surroundings, the comfy seats, the strident leftovers on people's plates.

'You're too soft for that kind of work,' I say.

He laughs instead of getting annoyed. He says, 'Maybe this is what getting older means, becoming disappointed in our own selves. And now I need to adjust to normal chitchat and the kind of everyday life where there isn't an urgent situation every two minutes. But I won't look for another job yet. I'll wait till my savings run out.'

He says that he's writing a story about a university professor. He begins to recite it out loud from memory: 'Hunched, the professor gazed into his glass of whiskey and slowly moved it round and round. The ice clinked. The professor said (and his voice was just a little slurred, his tone as if he was going to tell a secret) "I believe the earth is going to go round and round, round and round forever ... It will never stop."'

'Is that all?' I say. Through the window I can see the traffic building up. Bicycles weave among the black cabs.

'No, because his friend responds...'

'What friend?'

'There is a friend with him, his drinking companion.' Hisham says 'drinking companion' very slowly as if it is a foreign word. It is as if he wants to make a point about the distance he keeps from alcohol. He stresses each syllable, *drin-king com-pan-i-on*. 'He is writing a biography of Pascal,' Hisham adds with pride.

'Is he?'

'Yes and this is what he says to the professor when the professor says the earth will go round and round forever and never ever stop. He says – his voice is also just a bit slurred, but smoother – "My money is on it ending."'

'Then what,' I ask, my fingers reaching for my phone.

'That's it, that's my whole story. Don't you know Pascal's Wager?'

'No, I don't.'

'Pascal said that it is rational to wager that God exists because in doing that, you have everything to gain and nothing to lose. If you wager that He doesn't exist and then it turns out that He does, you lose everything. If you wager that He does exist and then it turns out that He doesn't, you won't lose anything.'

Hisham smiles and my brain works to catch up with him. He was like that too when he was young. I could never understand half of what he said or how he could possibly do things like listen to the Grateful Dead. And now he is drawing the Circle Line on a napkin.

I look down at the drawing. The Circle Line is not continuous. It does not go on and on in a loop. It has an end. 'This is the basic, deepest argument,' Hisham says. 'Will the world end or will it go on forever? Does time finish or not? A straight line starts at a certain point and ends at another, unless it goes on to infinity – and infinity must be a different place, not where the line started. But a circle promises continuity, round and round passing the same things. It makes sense to wager that the world – as we know it – will end.'

What he is saying doesn't sound new. 'Everyone knows that. What do you think people are doing every day?

Making the most of things before it's too late.'

'So they know already,' he says. 'It is that clear.'

In a way it is clear and in a way, it isn't. Through the window the buses look purposeful. Everyone's footsteps pound, beating out a march I can faintly hear. Come join this dance. Such beautiful shops ... and they're selling soft ice cream on the pavement. Eat, walk, shop, carry plastic bags, run and hop on to a bus. In the churn of central London, everyone is united by one wish. More to spend.

Is there nothing that everyone has, every single person?

I am surprised when Hisham answers, how sure he is. 'Time, everyone has time. But if the professor in my story is wrong and the earth stops going round and round, even time will stop.'

There is a message on my phone: my mother asking, 'What do think of Hisham?'

I could text back, 'Not sure' or 'so far, so good'. I ignore her instead. We walk out of the café. He falls in with my step. It matters that he does. It is significant, more appreciated than acknowledged. We walk past Hamleys and Liberty. We ignore the turn into Carnaby Street.

Eat, walk, shop, carry plastic bags, run and hop on to a bus. The truth is in the movement itself. Disappointment is embedded in every step. Because every beat takes us closer to the end. The world spins and there is hope. It is as if we are scooped up by a Ferris wheel that lifts us up, way up, in a circle, round, down and up.

Pages of Fruit

The first time I met you, not face to face, but through your words, was when I read *The Wedding Pistol* in an anthology of short stories written by women. This was back in the 1990s. To me, your voice was the most compelling, your story the only one transparent and in 3D. I remember I had my period while I was reading. It must have been the second or third day, after the tension and the cramps had subsided and what was left was the gentle steady flow. It relaxed me almost to the point of sleepiness. But I was not sleepy at all, I was fully alert to your voice, pulled down and immersed in the here and now of the pages in my hand. I gave in to the serene sense of my reproductive organs existing in passive mode, my days off, the secret celebration that I was not pregnant; another month's reprieve. I sank into the armchair, into myself and

I took your story understanding every reference, getting every joke. I hummed the tunes of songs you mentioned, I saw maps of the streets you pointed out. I was your perfect reader and I was too rapt to even stop and think that I don't want this to end.

This was the first time I recognised myself in fiction. Not my inner self, I was able to do that between the most unlikely covers, novels written by men from other centuries or set in places I didn't even know existed. But in your work I saw my country, my values and the social circles I grew up in. Of course I had read African literature before, the classics in which I recognised the people, weather, the landscape, the great panorama of life. But your story was different. Unashamedly you wrote about the top ten percent. A privileged childhood similar to mine. A highly educated family who could afford to travel to London for holidays and degrees. A family in which the children were brought up to dress, eat and speak differently (i.e. more Westernised) than their elders. I knew all about the outcome of this, the mixture of pride and opportunism; the growing impatience with needing to explain, the compulsion to stop and assign value.

I was in my twenties when I first read you, and I was voluble and impressionable. Immediately I wanted to be your friend. We had so much in common, both of us here and both of us from there, although you a decade older than me. I was eager to talk to you about your story; I felt that I already knew you and that sooner or later we would meet and the conversation would sparkle between us. Your story was a bridge to a world I had left behind after marriage and migration. A world I was losing, but through your words it became vivid again and I could inhabit it.

I wrote my first letter to you by hand and I do not have a copy. People, I am sure, had said to you, 'I devoured your novel', but your novel devoured me. The pain of the heroine became my pain, her conflicts more vivid than my existence. For days I neglected my children and husband. I saw them through glazed eyes; I sleepwalked through the housework. I was with you, not with them.

I dreamt of you (or your heroines, I am not sure, you were interchangeable). Happy dreams in which we sat side by side on stairs, like little girls. We didn't always speak about fiction, sometimes we swapped day to day experiences too – the school run, grumpy shop assistants, newspaper headlines – and your observations on life in the West chimed with mine. We were equals in spirit, our friendship based on shared experiences and ideas.

I continued to have variations of the same dream. The two of us on a seesaw, going up and down, both of us the same height, the same weight. The easy laughter between us, the words tumbling out of me. Telling you this and that. Repeating what I had already said in my letters or adding more. I would talk to you about my school friends, children and cousins and you knew them all already. They interested you for you hung on every word I said, threading in your own observations, details and insights specially formulated for me. You never needed me to introduce or to present, our conversations were an infinite continuation, a stream of goodwill. Even when the dream was over, the happiness and warmth remained with me infusing the day as if it were healing it.

You didn't reply to my letters. A year passed.

Your second novel made more of a splash. I cut out the reviews from the newspapers. But I noticed that even the good ones were patronising, few gave you your due. One did say 'a landmark' and I agreed. Better for me than the reviews were the interviews with you. A photo of you and your little girl on the beach. Your candid answers. Details of where you went to school and where you went to university – even your parents' careers. Such abundance, as generous as your prose. I now had so much to piece together, to match biography with fiction, to speculate, to double guess. In my plain, limited life you provided me with colour and adventure. I held you up as the epitome of intellect and glamour. The activity of reading and thinking about your work brought me hours of joy.

I spoke about you often to my husband and friends, who did not read your work, who were shocked by your progressive take and explicitness. The people around me were more conservative than the families in your books and your own family by extension. I had said that I responded to the familiarity of your characters and social circles, I had claimed them for myself. In truth, though, you and your characters inhabited the liberal fringes while I remained with the sedate majority. My parents and your parents would be acquaintances but never friends. They would have been members of the same club and been invited to the same parties but they would sit at different tables. My father would have heard of your father, the celebrated journalist. And your father would have bought his car from my father's Toyota agency. But your parents married for love, while mine had an arranged marriage. You studied in Britain as a child, while I came here as an adult. I have never smoked, drank alcohol or wore a bikini. If Westernisation was a linear progression and if assimilation was our ultimate goal (and that is debatable of course and not politically correct), but if either were true, then you were ahead of me by several steps. You belonged in Britain better than I did.

In my imaginary conversations with you and in my fan letters, I took you to task sometimes for your risqué scenes and the sinful behaviour of your heroines. Hopefully you didn't misunderstand me, I was neither aggressive nor didactic. My tone was gently mocking, a tut tut. It would be dishonest not to admit that your explicit love scenes added to the allure of your work. Besides, I enjoyed the bristle in my mind in accommodating your liberal stance. But in my day-to-day life, I was as restrained and conventional as the people around me.

Was your life, and the daring lives of your characters, the life I longed for? In school, I had known outgoing girls similar to your younger heroines. Girls who were brimming with confidence, unencumbered by shyness. They had boyfriends who rode motorcycles and they dabbled in weed and unchaperoned meetings. These girls glittered out of my reach. I ached for recognition from them – one of my diary entries at the age of thirteen reads, 'What I want is that when they are asked who this girl (me) is, their answer would be this is so and so, she is quite nice but I don't know her very well. This is not what is happening now. They don't even know my name!' Your heroines are a resurrection of those sparkling girls who I was invisible to. So you see, your writing did not transport me to another world but instead welcomed me into conversations and outings that had been barred to me. It was as if, in the reading, I were mixing with people who had at one time brushed past me. Thank you for this access.

And for being there for me when I came out of hospital – once the painkillers had worn off, your paperback was the alternative drug. When we moved house – putting your hardback up on the new shelves from John Lewis. When I had the miscarriage – one of the nurses was also called Selma. When I got my first laptop – typing you a letter. When my father passed away – his funeral exactly like the one you described. When I enrolled in the Open University and told you about it in a letter. When we went on holiday to Barcelona and I came across *Frutos de Loto* in a bookshop near the hotel. I had written about *Fruit*

Lotus, my favourite of all your novels, to the Richard and Judy Book Club when they first started asking for viewer recommendations. In those years you were often unfairly overlooked, consistently underrated. I was one of your early champions, long before you became mainstream.

I searched for you in the early days of the Internet. Even before Google, I put your name in AltaVista and Ask Jeeves. The first email I sent you, I signed 'Your fan from Aberdeen'. I always used this signature so that I would stand out and be remembered. 'Ah', I imagined you saying with fondness, 'that lady again from North Scotland.' Perhaps you would also be proud that you were read so far north, though, over the years and with your growing success, you might have started taking a larger readership for granted. I wrote to you about my parents' divorce. I cringe now when I reread this email and intend to delete it. (I will delete them all). When I wrote that first email my husband was away on business, my youngest child was ill with fever and it was a public holiday so I couldn't get him to the doctor. My period was late and I was holding my breath, anxious that I was pregnant again. To make matters worse I was also getting obscene anonymous phone calls so upsetting that every time the phone rang, my blood ran cold. Because I couldn't sleep I wrote to you about my mother.

The toddler with the rasping hot breath tossing next to me, the phone off the hook, my body on high alert for the first sign of my late period – the women in your novels don't go through these things. They are not always in control but still, their will is strong and their confidence high. They triumph and they surge forward climbing mountains, confronting riot police, filming a lioness giving birth. My mother resembled your heroines. I elaborated on that in the email. She was outspoken and vibrant, the kind of person everyone agreed was ahead of her time. She left my father because he stifled her. She walked out on us and struck out on her own, supporting herself and fulfilling her potential. My mother's story would not have shocked you. You understood that the West's image of 'the Muslim woman' was a reduced, simplified cliché. My mother was neither more nor less Muslim than others, she was different because of her personality, education and more significantly her independent means. In my email, I showed off about her because I couldn't show off about myself. I couldn't write down how fervently I was praying for my period to come, for my husband to return, for my son's fever to break. Instead I spoke of my mother standing up to society and how pioneering she was. I glossed over the abandoned child (me) running after the car, my father vomiting through the night, the scathing things people said. I told you that she, like you, was an inspiration to me. That night I dreamt of a woman who was my mother and who was you at the same time. She hugged me and I wept with relief.

Your feminism and that of my mother's was of a similar kind, birthed in one city with the same influences. It meant birth control, work outside the home, and a refusal to be bogged down by either convention or religion. This particular kind of feminism could not accommodate sisterhood. Other women were to be climbed upon to get to the top and it did not mean compassion because that was a weakness. I was a disappointment to my mother while at the same time fulfilling her prophecy that without her upbringing I was doomed. She sacrificed me. These were here words, not mine. She was content to have a daughter who was lesser than her. You might want to write about my mother. Her anguish (or not) at having to leave her child. We were the noose that hung around her neck – her words not mine. I did, once, ask my mother why she did not take me with her. And she smiled sadly because my question betrayed my stupidity. She had wanted to leave me as much as she had wanted to leave my father.

The first time I travelled to see you was a big deal for me. I had never travelled alone. Would you believe it? I was twenty-eight and I had never travelled alone. He asked me, why do you really want to go? What are you going to do there? What are you going to gain? I had to answer these questions in order to get the necessary green light. Weeks of preparing babysitters and meals, sorting out all the logistics. I bought a new outfit, I went on a crash diet, I splurged on a facial. The finances were an issue all to themselves. There was the return train ticket to Edinburgh, the ticket to your event, the cost of your new hardback which I would surely buy and stand proudly in the queue to get signed. Why proudly? Because I had been your fan for years and because it would be my first ever time to speak to a writer. I would only queue for you and no one else, believe me.

Naturally I didn't sleep the night before. All the growing excitement, the false alarms that flared up to threaten my outing. At the station, seeing an ad for the Edinburgh International Book Festival with your name on it made my palms turn cold. I hadn't prepared myself for missing the children. My wrong empty lap, the Kit Kat I couldn't share and all the sights that rolled past my window – but it would have been intolerable to have you in Scotland and not be there to welcome you.

Charlotte Square was busy with sun, wind, tents and people of all ages. Having traversed such a wide distance (metaphorically speaking), I was suddenly filled with a sense of urgency. I had to immediately find you. I walked into the Authors Tent. You were moving the first time I saw you. A buffet was laid out and you whisked through it, stabbing your choices, knowing exactly what you wanted, filling your plate with efficiency. You were as beautiful as I had imagined except for that extra energy, a fire that didn't show in photographs, almost a jerkiness. I went up to you as you were twisting away from the table, greeted you like a friend. You stopped as if I were blocking you, you stiffened at my familiarity, my presumption. 'Are you a writer?' Before I could answer, your eyes scanned my face, flickered over my clothes. It had seemed to me a miracle that I managed to get myself out of the house without a child's grubby hands leaving a mark on my new skirt or a splatter of Ribena. But faced with your effortless elegance, my new Marks & Spencer outfit felt clunky. And all too soon you had already judged me. I said, 'I am your fan from Aberdeen. I write to you…' You noted my accent, your novelist's eyes picked up the signs of early marriage, abandoned university degree, rampant fertility. 'This is the Authors Tent,' you said moving away not to join a group or to be claimed by someone else. I was shaken by only one thought – all the letters I had written to you over the years, all the emails, meant nothing to you. You've never read a single word I've written.

I walked out to the deckchairs and ice creams, the good-natured crowd who knew how to behave. They had read more books than me and met more writers. I almost headed to the train station but common sense prevailed and I decided to attend your talk as planned.

During the event you made me proud, speaking with intelligence and a vulnerability I had not expected. The audience was mainly female. As you were being led outside, I heard one of them say, 'She's very attractive.' I immediately wanted to tell you about this. I imagined us sitting at one of the tables that were scattered over the grass, our coffees between us. I imagined your relief that your session was over. But I knew even as the fantasy formed clearly in my mind, that it wouldn't happen. You would not sit with me. I bought your new novel but I did not queue for the book signing.

I took the train back to Aberdeen. My pain was exaggerated but real. No heroine of yours would travel, as I did, back by train and into the arms of her husband and children, abashed and broken, regretful that she had ventured out. In terms of the unwritten rules of the housewife, I had taken a 'day off'. An expensive one at that. The expectation was that I would resume my duties refreshed and in good spirits. Instead I moped around the house analysing the failure of our meeting.

I combed your novels and the answers were in your work. The digs at the women who wore hijab. Such women were never, God-forbid, the heroines or even friends or relatives of the heroines but only jolly servants or passers-by. I had never taken these digs seriously before. We have so much in common, I wailed to your receding back. Could you not look beyond the hijab?

The prize nomination, all those white people queuing to hear you speak, the four-star reviews of your latest paperback must have all gone to your head. It had given you delusions of grandeur and made you look down on your own kind. We had become mere fodder for your fiction, you would use our lives but not grant us your company. Yes, I should laugh the whole thing off. Or, as a modern consumer deprive you of my custom because of your poor client treatment. There were other writers waiting to be read.

Weeks later I still buzzed occasionally with injustice

but the hurt diminished with each passing day. A new pregnancy pushed you completely to the back of my mind. A new school for the children, my husband's promotion. A year passed and then more. My family were growing and I took pride and care in the children's lives. My sons, taller than me now, engaged with me more as semi-independent adults than needy children. My two little girls, alike but not alike, were absorbing. I delighted in their closeness to each other, their intimate infinite friendship. Sometimes seeing them sitting on the stairs side by side whispering or perfectly balanced on either side of a seesaw, I would remember, fleetingly, my dreams of us. But I no longer wrote to you.

Once in a while, though, I googled your name as if checking up on an old friend. Your career had taken another direction. You started to write for children. You teamed up with your brother, the artist, and wrote picture books in which you upgraded the *One Thousand and One Nights* for a modern, technologically savvy global readership. I admired you for working with your brother. It showed how authentic you were, still tied to our family values. Actually, I only bought one of your new books, the one modelled on *Ali Baba and the Forty Thieves*. By then my sons were too old and my daughters' preferred the Power Puff Girls. (This was long before you wrote *Sindy, the Sailor*, the modern female incarnation of Sindbad). When the twins were very young they rejected anything that had a whiff of African or Muslim culture about it

– including your books. This disappointed me because I wanted them to have pride in their heritage. Thankfully, it was a phase and they got over it as they became older and more conscious.

The birth of the twins had been a watershed for me. I was determined not to have any more children and to complete my distance learning degree. To be honest, I still raised the radio's volume when you were interviewed on Woman's Hour, I still admired your new hairstyle in that photo in *The Telegraph*, but my interest had lost its edge.

* * *

The next time I met you was fifteen years later, in Abu Dhabi. We had moved for my husband's work and after settling in, I too found a job. I became first an assistant then a coordinator in an educational non-profit foundation which promoted a love of reading among children. My life changed when I started to earn my own money. I could now afford a part-time maid and to pay for the children's school bus. Freed from the weight of the school run and the bulk of the housework, I poured myself into my new job and I began to enjoy myself. To take delight in the malls and the beach. I relaxed in this family oriented environment, where children stayed up late and the pace of life was slower.

Your name came up often in the course of my work. The early taboo-breaking novels were now forgotten – some of them were out of print and not available on Kindle. You were now famous for your wholesome children's books. Her Highness, Sheikha Hadia, the CEO of our foundation, spoke of them highly. I liked Sheikha Hadia for her direct warmth and her unselfconsciousness. In her black abaya and designer sunglasses, she possessed a can-do attitude that was combined with informality. During meetings, she would fiddle with her phone, wipe her fingers with Wet Wipes or slide her feet out of her sandals and rub them against the carpet. Once I came across her in the prayer room, undistinguishable among the bowing staff and the cleaners.

An invitation was issued for you to visit the Emirate. Sheikha Hadia wanted you to visit seven schools, to whom we would distribute free copies of your books. The week it took you to reply coincided with my mother's visit. After years of not seeing her, I strained for approval and spent considerable time, effort and expense in showing off. She had in the past openly expressed her disapproval of the core elements of my life, so I was overjoyed when Abu Dhabi appealed to her. She admired the children's international school, she was impressed with the compound we were living in and by extension my husband and his work for providing such excellent housing. Best of all, though, was how pleasantly surprised and admiring she was of my job. 'It took you ages,' she said, 'but you've finally made something of yourself! I had written you off.' Such praise threaded in scorn did hurt and once or twice I hid in the bathroom and cried. But I was relieved that I had risen in her estimation and that our relationship was warmer than it had ever been. Outwardly, I handled the visit well, without a single mishap or argument. This control must have taken its toll, though, because when she left, I took the afternoon off and spent the rest of the day in bed too fatigued to even get up and cook.

I did not feel sad or depressed. Only like a machine temporarily switched off. In *Fruit Lotus*, your most poignant novel in my opinion, a husband stops loving his wife. Just like that. It is fascinating, I agree, how love can come to an end, how it can just stop like the gush of a tap ceasing, like a long night surfacing up to a dawn, like sweetness lingering on the tongue then vanishing. The fictional husband does not leave his wife for someone else but we know that by the end of the novel, he will. You spare us the details, you are subtle but we know that the treachery is round the corner. No longer loving the heroine, he is open and primed for a fresh adventure while she soldiers on with the children and the blow to her femininity.

You pulled me out of this temporary setback with an email saying how delighted you would be to visit Abu Dhabi and how fervently you supported the foundation's aim. I found myself approving the Business Class tickets on Etihad, the booking of the five-star hotel and the chauffeur driven car. I personally answered your email queries on the availability of free Wi-Fi in your room. In

addition to the school visits, we were also holding a one-
day seminar on writing for children, in which you would
give the opening speech. We scheduled for you a special
dinner with the Sheikha. All other meals were provided at
the magnificent Emirates Palace Hotel.

You did not remember me or the fan mail I had long
ago sent. I didn't expect you to. I was a different woman
now, older and more confident. You, too, were heavier
looking. Despite your dyed hair, there were tender bags
under your eyes and your deep smoker's voice aged you.
But you were still beautiful and vibrant. Compared to
Edinburgh, there was a relaxed good will about you. Abu
Dhabi pleased you – this desert miracle, a futuristic world
of optimism and lavish expansion. You singled me out as
the only one in the foundation who was from your home
country. Years ago I had longed for this connection. And
now here it was.

Privately, we spoke in our dialect; a few times we
exchanged knowing glances and inside jokes. All mild and
relating to work – but it was enough for me. That old wish
to be your friend flickered. And holding this together was
my pride in how much I had achieved since that day in
Edinburgh. When I spoke of my admiration for your early
novels, I did so without belittling myself. I never referred
to my letters of long ago. I was mature and professional.
Too senior in the foundation to accompany you on every
school visit, I met you at the more official events including
the dinners. Privately, I chaffed a little at this. Sitting in

the car, negotiated the heavy traffic from one school to the next, would certainly have meant spending more time with you but Sheikha Hadia was demanding my full attention. The success of your visit had long term consequences for the foundation; the favourable response of our company sponsors, the local media and the Ministry of Education were our primary focus.

I admit that as a foundation, we did spring upon you the children's writing workshop. I am sorry that despite your objections, I insisted on going ahead. To quell your rebellion, I invited your publisher's Middle East Sales Representative, who was based in Dubai, to come to the workshop and threw in an overnight stay for him, his wife and toddler at the Beach Rotana. His role would be to remind you of how your visit was impacting on the sales of your books to the extent that your delighted publishers in London were reprinting.

My strategy worked. But only just. After huffing and puffing, you seated yourself in front of the children. You made a few general comments about writing and the importance of books. All excellent points that pleased Sheikha Hadia. Then it was time for the children to read out their stories to you. Head bowed over an open notebook, you doodled dark angular lines; you drew prison bars, broken wings and shaded faces. I could see them because I was sitting next to you, as if symbolically hemming you in so you would not abscond! You drew knotted wool and crooked wire; steel scourer and patterned grids. You doodled with rage, flinching from what you were hearing. You did not, once, look up at the stuttering child struggling to read what he had written, the one swaying side to side chanting a rhyme she had made up, the serious boy who had no concept of grammar.

Worst was to come when the children lined up for you to sign their books – the ones the foundation had distributed to them for free. To be honest, they didn't really line up, they were all over the place, pretty noisy, shoving the books under your nose, elbowing each other out of the way. When one of them pushed a copy of *The Very Hungry Caterpillar* under your nose, you lost your temper. 'That's not my book,' you lashed out. 'I won't sign a book that's not mine!' With an agility I thought I had lost, I rose from my seat, grabbed a copy of *Ali and the Forty Baddies* and placed it instead into the girl's hand. I removed the offending *Hungry Caterpillar* from under your nose. Things went more or less smoothly after that.

* * *

It was your last night in Abu Dhabi, the special dinner with Sheikha Hadia that had taken so long to organise. I sat next to her with you on the other side. The atmosphere was relaxed and so were you. You spoke at length about your brother, the artist who collaborated on your books. It occurred to me that you might have been under family pressure to help him with his career. I admired you for promoting him in front of the Sheikha. She was accustomed to people asking favours of her. Some needed jobs, residence visas or referrals. She was primed for this and though you were not at all forthcoming in making any specific requests, the ground was set for the future. Next time we, as a foundation, would most likely invite your brother as well.

Sheikha Hadia, as was her habit, wiped her fingers with Wet Wipes in between courses. She would open her handbag, take out the packet, peel it open and slowly remove a scented wet cloth. The scent used to be amber but now, it seemed, she had switched to an alcohol free, antibacterial. I was used to her habit and sometimes even concerned that it implied an obsessive-compulsive disorder. So I was taken aback, when after she left the dinner, you made a slight dig about it. A whisper aside, aimed only at me, said in our dialect. Perhaps your disdain of the hijab, less obvious to me now than it had been that time in Edinburgh, extended to the Sheikha's flowing, black abaya. I smiled at your witty remark but my heart wasn't in it.

'I need a cigarette,' you said as the rest of us got up from the table. 'Anyone care to join me outside?'

I volunteered to go with you. We walked out of the hotel through a side door that opened out onto a slip road and further ahead was the busy motorway. In contrast to the cold air conditioner inside, it was humid and still. The air was full of car fumes. They shimmered suspended over the gleaming cars waiting for the valet parking. The hotel porters walked back and forth wearing a heavy, theatrical uniform unsuitable for the weather.

You looked relieved that you were flying back home tomorrow. Jaunty as you took your cigarette box out of your handbag. 'You don't smoke? I can tell you're not the type.'

I shook my head. You were already lighting up. True, I was not the type. But still your words had the hint of a put down, an unnecessary insistence that we were different. I had been slow to understand what you intuited that first day in Edinburgh. That we would never become friends.

It was my turn now to look at you with eyes that were not a novelist's eyes. I saw that you were beautiful but not sexy, more talented than blessed, brittle but not weighty. And I was your opposite. I said, 'I hope you enjoyed your time here.'

Your reply was the same one I had heard this morning on the local radio. The exact wording. Except that you now added how your mother, a gynaecologist, worked here in the 1970s and delivered a prince. This was not new to me either. I had read about it in your piece about your mother's work in O, *The Oprah Magazine*.

I asked only because I could. 'Do you ever read your fan mail?'

'From the children?'

'From readers in general.'

You shrugged. 'I'm not an agony aunt. And I don't

want to be told "write about me" either.'

You had said these exact words before in an interview, 'I'm not an agony aunt.' Although you were lifting the cigarette to your lips, I felt as if I were in the presence of a statue, one that was opaque and unyielding. It made me miss the voice on the page, the fluid lives you had written down.

There was nothing more that I could take from you. Nothing in addition to what I already had on my shelves.

Later, I went home and instead of checking up on the children, instead of tackling the kitchen or setting the table for tomorrow's breakfast, I got into bed and started to read, again, my favourite novel.

Acknowledgements

I am forever indebted to Elisabeth Schmitz, my editor at Grove, for supporting every single one of my books and for her encouragement and belief in me over the years. My thanks also go to Deb Seager, Jazmine Goguen and Katie Raissian.

I am very grateful to Lynn Gaspard at Saqi Books for offering to publish this collection which brings together the first stories I ever wrote –'Coloured Lights' and 'The Ostrich'– as well as more recent ones –'The Circle Line' and 'Pages of Fruit'.

In reviewing the stories, I was conscious of all who had helped me throughout the years and the debt of gratitude I owe them.

My husband, Nadir Mahjoub, my first reader, has supported and encouraged me without any hesitation, even when I 'threatened' many times to give up writing.

I am grateful to the very first Caine Prize judging panel, the chair Ben Okri as well as Veronique Tadjo, William Boyd and the late Professor Alvaro Ribeiro for choosing 'The Museum' as the winner. It would not have reached their hands had it not been submitted by the champion of African writing, Becky Nana Ayebia Clarke, to whom I, and many others, owe a great deal.

For feedback on early drafts and for getting me to take writing seriously, I am grateful to Todd McEwen who in the early 1990s was writer-in-residence at Aberdeen Central Library.

Many thanks too to my friend Irene Leake for her creative insight and positivity.

I am grateful to all the editors and the publications in which these stories first appeared:

'The Museum' in *Opening Spaces* edited by Yvonne Vera (Heinemann AWS, 1999)

'Majed' in *Wasafiri Magazine* (2000)

'Coloured Lights', 'Souvenirs', 'The Ostrich,' and 'The Boy from the Kebab Shop' in my collection *Coloured Lights* (Polygon, 2001)

'Something Old, Something New' in *Scottish Girls About Town* (Pocket Books, 2003)

'Farida's Eyes' in *Banipal 44* (2012)

'Summer Maze' in *Jalada Transition, the Fear Issue* (2017)

'The Circle Line' in *Gulf Coast Magazine* (2017)

'Pages of Fruit' in *Freeman's Home* (Grove Press, 2017)